The Day Always Comes

Also by Richard Osborn

Til Death Do Us Part

The Day Always Comes

Richard Osborn

ARCHWAY PUBLISHING

Copyright © 2016, 2017 Richard Osborn.

All rights reserved. No part of this book may be used or reproduced by any means, graphic, electronic, or mechanical, including photocopying, recording, taping or by any information storage retrieval system without the written permission of the author except in the case of brief quotations embodied in critical articles and reviews.

This is a work of fiction. All of the characters, names, incidents, organizations, and dialogue in this novel are either the products of the author's imagination or are used fictitiously.

Archway Publishing books may be ordered through booksellers or by contacting:

Archway Publishing
1663 Liberty Drive
Bloomington, IN 47403
www.archwaypublishing.com
1 (888) 242-5904

Because of the dynamic nature of the Internet, any web addresses or links contained in this book may have changed since publication and may no longer be valid. The views expressed in this work are solely those of the author and do not necessarily reflect the views of the publisher, and the publisher hereby disclaims any responsibility for them.

Any people depicted in stock imagery provided by Thinkstock are models, and such images are being used for illustrative purposes only.
Certain stock imagery © Thinkstock.

ISBN: 978-1-4808-4399-8 (sc)
ISBN: 978-1-4808-4400-1 (e)

Library of Congress Control Number: 2017903449

Print information available on the last page.

Archway Publishing rev. date: 04/17/2017

To
My literary friends

Everyone has to start somewhere.
Remind yourself of this as you look at those
who have what you'd like to have.
It may seem very far away at this point,
but if you keep going, your day will come.
—Holiday Mathis

Acknowledgments

I am grateful to two people who diligently helped me in the final stages of this story. Their expertise brought to my attention words and phrases, which needed work.

Linda Millette lives in Maryland and was a great help in the timeline, punctuation, and typos department. Nothing went past her eyes. She is an experienced catchall editor.

My wife, Tish, lives with me in Edina, Minnesota, and we're celebrating fifty years of marriage. She read my manuscript and gave me feedback from a reader's point of view. She worked tirelessly. Even when she couldn't sleep, she would get up in the night and read the manuscript. I love her dearly for her helping hand, great feedback, and encouragement.

I thank you both. Even though they had many suggestions, my story did not become their story.

Prologue

John Logan grew up in a family of six. He was the oldest of two boys and two girls. His father, Ned, a self-made man, had a talent for interior design, reconstruction, painting, and wallpapering. He kept a firm grip on the family, especially the two boys, but in a different way, he had great affection for his two daughters. John's mother, Marie, worked at home as a homemaker, the usual occupation of a woman in the '50s, cooking, cleaning, and doing the laundry. She realized the importance of raising the family with Ned's support. His work provided a comfortable income for their modest home. They weren't rich, but they weren't poor. They were a happy family.

John never had a room of his own, having to share a bedroom with his brother. Each of the four went on to college with scholarships, worked part-time, and provided for themselves. John started at an early age in high school and worked with his father through college in the summer months, as well as during winter and spring breaks.

John graduated magna cum laude from the University of Michigan with a degree in civil engineering and gained employment with a firm in the city. The work seemed like drudgery because he had a love for his father's occupation. He couldn't shake the feeling of wanting to paint, wallpaper, remodel and satisfy the desire to follow in his father's footsteps. After two long years of city work, John decided he would go into business with his father and eventually be on his own after his dad retired.

Dianne had come into John's life while they were in college. They dated for almost the entire four years and a year after graduation John and Dianne married.

Father Jim Fisher was John and Dianne's parish priest, a family friend, and a high school classmate. Jim and John had been close for more than twenty years. Father Jim married John and Dianne, and yes, she spelled her name with two n's—which always caused confusion. Father Jim baptized their two daughters. He had been John's confessor, friend, and confidant. The two men had jogged together, played tennis, and were golfing partners before John and Dianne married.

One evening, as per usual, John was jogging and passed Nancy Moore's home on the corner of Chestnut and Grand. Nancy was in the driveway getting out of her car, having arrived home from work. John and Nancy knew each other well and usually volunteered together on weekends at a food shelf. It was winter, and the driveway appeared slippery, so John went up to help her into the house with some packages.

Nancy noticed the back storm door was slightly open. She thought she had pulled it tight, and it would lock behind her when she had it armed, but she couldn't remember if she did arm it. She mentioned her mistake to John but insisted she must have left it ajar. Laughing at her absent-mindedness as of late, John insisted on going in and checking things out before she entered.

John came back and said the house looked fine, with no evidence of a break-in, and offered her his hand to help her come in. Nancy started to slip because of the ice and John grabbed her arm. Had he not grabbed her, she would have fallen. Her skin was warm, and his grab was firm, making a mark of his fingernails on her wrist. He apologized, but Nancy assured him if he had not caught her, she could have seriously injured herself. They went inside, and John stayed a moment, put some chapstick on his lips rubbing his index finger on them to spread the lip salve evenly. Nancy was so excited to show him what she had bought. It was a scarf from Hermes of Paris; a limited design. She had quite a fetish for scarfs, so she put it on around her neck. John poured himself a glass of water, went into the living room with Nancy and looked in the mirror. John thought it was beautiful. He put the empty glass on the table in front of the mirror and helped her to adjust the scarf. They planned to meet on Saturday morning to go to the volunteer workplace. John left.

Nancy Moore did not report to work the next morning. The office personnel thought she was ill and remarked it was strange she hadn't called. She always did. The following day came, and when Nancy didn't show again, her supervisor called her home with no answer. They suspected something was wrong and reported it to the police.

When the police arrived, the back door was unlocked. Upon entering, they found her lying between the dining room door and the kitchen entrance. She was not responsive. They called an ambulance and took her to the local hospital emergency room. The doctor on duty pronounced her dead on arrival.

The next day, the coroner reported she had been dead for roughly twenty-four to forty-eight hours because the autopsy revealed she had not eaten an evening meal or breakfast the next morning. The marks on her neck suggested Nancy Moore died of strangulation. A mark on her wrist appeared prominently with the police thinking it appeared someone grabbed her. An empty bag from Saks Fifth Avenue lay next to her body with a sales slip dated two days earlier. It identified a scarf she had bought; it was not there.

Two people had seen a man running from Nancy's house around five-forty-five on that dark February evening. Their story was consistent. The incriminating evidence was a broken water glass clearly showing fingerprints and lip impression. The mark left on Nancy's arm from John, grabbing her so she didn't fall, also became evidence. After the glass had been examined at the police lab, they determined the match was John Logan's. There was enough residue of lip imprint and fingerprints from the person who drank from it to conduct a DNA test. John always puts lip balm on when he went running, especially in the winter. The DNA of the lip print was also a match with John. He was arrested on 1st-degree murder charges.

Six months later the trial began and the two witnesses stuck to their story, insisting they had seen a man running from Nancy's house two evenings before her body was discovered and he had slipped and fallen. He was wearing a white, hooded sweatshirt. It was dark, making it difficult to look at the individual's face, so they were unable to identify the person. They assumed it was a man. The only physical evidence was the broken glass, the mark on Nancy's arm, the lip balm imprint, the white hooded sweatshirt, and the DNA.

The trial lasted two weeks. The prosecution presented the case from the physical evidence of fingerprints, DNA from the lip print on the glass, the mark on her arm, and the couple seeing a man running from Nancy's house. The defense presented the question of the gender of the person the couple saw. They couldn't tell if it was a man or a woman; it was dark. The defense also introduced the fact that Nancy and John were good friends and there was no intimate contact between them. John's wife Dianne took the witness stand to support him. She did not ever think they were anything but good friends.

The broken glass and the DNA did not help John's defense. A search warrant of John and Dianne's home produced the discovery of a white, hooded sweatshirt in John's closet and the lip balm he frequently used. The prosecutors already had pieces of physical evidence against him, and also the couple who insisted it was a man. However, the defense could not prove otherwise, so the jury believed the evidence and the prosecution's case.

On the day the trial ended, six hours later the jury entered the courtroom with a verdict. The twelve jurors found John guilty and recommended to the judge he receive the death penalty.

She agreed and sentenced him to death by lethal injection.

1

Sharon Gibbons reached for the bottle of Tylenol. Each capsule was extra strength, 500 mg. The bottle originally contained 225 tablets and was half empty. She downed four on an empty stomach. Her headache of more than several days had become intense. She knew she needed to get some help.

"Mike, come for your breakfast. We have to go."

No answer.

"Michael, it's eight fifteen. I have to get you to daycare by nine o'clock."

No answer.

"Michael John Gibbons. Where are you?"

Sharon walked to the staircase leading to the basement. She only called him Michael including his middle name when she needed him *pronto*. Otherwise, he was Mike. Still no answer. Sharon walked into the living room and stopped at the bottom of the stairs leading to the second floor. She was about to call him again.

"Hi, Mama."

Michael was standing at the top of the stairs but dressed and as usual, shoeless.

"Please get down here so we can get going, and bring your shoes. Your breakfast cereal is on the table. Besides, I still have this headache; it's driving me crazy. I'm going to the urgent care clinic this afternoon.

Grandma Louise and Grandpa Eli are coming for the weekend from Ohio. I'm going to ask them to pick you up today."

"Okay, Mama. I come right now."

Mike came down the stairs, sat down, and started to put a shoe on the wrong foot.

"Honestly, Mike." Sharon smiled. "I've told you and showed you several times which foot your shoes go on."

"I know, Mama, but I get confused. Does it matter which foot? They both fit good on either foot."

Mike put his shoes on the proper foot. Sharon decided it would be quicker if she tied them herself. He knew how to do it. He'd learned it quickly, but it took him forever because he used his dominant left hand. "For a four-year-old, you're doing very well. I didn't have to dress you this morning, even though your shirt doesn't match your pants."

"But I like this shirt. And these pants are my favorites."

Sharon smiled, ruffled his hair, and put on her coat. The headaches were too often. A week ago, they'd come and gone, but now, mostly, they stayed. Sometimes her eyeballs ached, and light was intolerable. She wore her sunglasses nearly all the time. Mike sat down, ate his cereal, put his dish in the sink, and put on his jacket.

They left the house and headed for the car in the garage. Mike jumped in the back seat and into his car seat, and he was able to secure his seat belt, shoulder harness, and crotch buckle. Sharon checked the connections.

"Good job, Mike. You're getting to be pretty self-sufficient."

"Thanks, Mama, but what does self-fasisient mean?"

His mom smiled and said, "It means, as I said, you're doing very well." She gave him a kiss.

Sharon got in, started the car, and backed out. The morning traffic was its usual heavy volume. Her headache didn't help, but she would get to daycare before nine. When they arrived, Mike waited for his mom to undo his seat belts as he'd been taught. Sharon kissed him good-bye. He ran inside, and turning, he waved, raising his left hand and arm from the window.

How did he get a dominate left hand? Sharon wondered. *Probably from his father.*

She got back into the car and started it. *Oh, this headache,* she thought as she drove away. The sun shining in her eyes was intense. She decided to stop by the clinic right now before going to work.

She accelerated on the entrance ramp to the speed limit and blended into the other traffic. Suddenly, her head fell forward, her chin to her chest. At the curve ahead, her car continued straight ahead and left the road. She apparently never saw the tree in front of her. She was going at least sixty miles per hour when the impact occurred; the air bags activated. She had her seat belt on, and it held her body in place. The horn sounded continuously.

※

"Nine-One-One, what is your emergency?"

"A car hit a tree at high speed on Forrester Road and M-21."

"Can you tell how many are in the car?"

"I don't know. It looks like just one."

"I've dispatched the emergency vehicles. They should be there within five minutes. Thank you for the call."

※

The police, ambulance, and necessary equipment arrived, and the EMTs suspected when they saw Sharon that she had not survived. The man who had seen the accident and had called 9-1-1 was driving behind her. He told the police the car had never slowed down, and the brake lights had never come on.

A few days later, the autopsy report revealed Sharon had died of an intracranial aneurysm.

2

After his mother's death, Mike went to live with his grandparents in Ohio. His grandfather died three years later, so he continued to be raised by his grandmother. He was now eighteen, a senior in high school, and captain of the wrestling team, popular and well-liked by his classmates and friends. With the wrestling season over in late January, he pledged, on the advice of his coach, to stay in shape. He had lost his final wrestling match to his most feared opponent earlier in the month. He was always the rival who gave Mike the most struggles in the competitive sport. During the final match, Mike watched every move of his opponent, the shuffle left and shuffle right carefully choreographed. Being left-handed, it seemed he had an advantage over the mostly right-handed opponents. When the time came, Mike was ready to push right, and then, if all went well, it would be over, but it didn't happen. Mike's opponent caught him off balance and slammed him down to the mat. His opponent earned the two-point takedown. The buzzer sounded, signaling the match was over. Mike had lost.

Had he won, he would have been the all-time champion in wrestling at the school. He was angry about his defeat. He was angry about a lot of his life so far—his mother's death, not knowing who his father was, and now his loss of the final wrestling match of his senior year. His having been conceived through artificial insemination and the circumstances of his mother's death were common knowledge. He had an angry disposition, a result of holding the emotions connected to everything he had gone through inside. He tried to stop thinking about his mother's death and life's unfairness, but memories of the day she had died would often come back to haunt him. He was only four at the time but had a memory of something happening to her.

It started in his early years when kids would ask him where his father was. His friends and playmates would tease him about his grandmother and why he referred to her as "Mom." So Mike decided just to call her Grandma.

Mike took up wrestling in the sixth grade, and his coach, through observation, approached him about his anger issues. The coach said wrestling would be good in several ways and would help move him beyond his anger through aggressive response. He impressed with young Mike that this didn't mean being pushy or demanding; it meant being respectful of yourself and others. He talked to him about good and evil, right and wrong, and how they will come into your life. You had to decide on how to respond to them, and then have to live through each of these. Later, as they came to know one another, the coach gave Mike some meditation CDs on various topics, anger being one of them. Mike respected his coach because the coach understood him, but Mike couldn't apprehend why people would meditate at all. He started listening to the CDs, but they made little sense to him. He listened to the "how to" instructions and started a regular time taking time each day to sit, relax, and listen. Then one day after several months, Mike decided maybe they were helping to lessen his anxiety, irritability, moodiness, and a host of other feelings, but mostly, they allowed him to relax.

It was early February in northern Ohio. The days were dark, and the sunset early, with the temperatures cold but tolerable. Mike bundled up in his long underwear and his heavy sweatpants. Two sweatshirts were in order. As he left the house at about five, he told his grandmother he would be back in about an hour.

Louise knew Mike liked his late-afternoon runs. It helped delay his appetite. As he was about to leave, Grandma Louise said, "I wish you wouldn't go out so late. The area you go to is not the best. You know there was a murder committed at Chestnut and Grand recently. It was at Nancy Moore's place. I knew who she was at church but never met her. I think the area's unsafe. Cars can't always see you, and if you slipped on an icy surface, you could break a leg, or worse yet, hit your—"

"I know, I know, Grandma," Mike interrupted. "I'll be fine. Besides, they caught the man who did it. It was that John Logan guy. His trial is over, and his sentence will come soon. They're seeking the death penalty."

Mike hesitated, putting his head down and closing his eyes, but he continued, "So don't worry, Grandma. I go over to the track next to the baseball field, mostly ground cinders, and even with snow on it, there's good traction. I'll be fine and back for dinner. I do pass the house where the murder was committed, and I look at it. I think about it, but there are usually lights on inside, and I feel safe. Please don't worry."

"I can't help it. I knew the Logan family. I remember John Logan when they were at church. I believe he followed his father's footsteps. What a tragedy."

"Okay, I hear you, Grandma. But I can't help it. I like to run just before dinner." Mike came over and gave her a kiss on the cheek. "I love you, Grandma."

Grandma Louise smiled, looked at Mike, and said, "I love you too, Mike."

Mike returned a little later than usual, and dinner was ready.

During his run, Mike had decided it was best not to go so late. He realized how it upset his grandmother, and he didn't like doing it to her. He loved her; she was his mom, no matter what anyone else thought.

Grandma said, "I'm glad you're back. See, it took you longer. With your graduation coming up in June, I would hate to see some injury happen to you."

"I walked around the track before I started the run to check for ice."

Grandma Louise had the dinner ready, and they sat down together.

"I wish you would go to the college and inquire if you could run in the field house. It would be warm, and you wouldn't have to wear all that heavy clothing. Besides, you could probably shower there after you finish. You could also take the VW with you for safety reasons. And best of all, no snow or ice."

Mike listened to his grandma. She spoke in a higher tone of voice, moving her fork in her hand as she was speaking. Grandma Louise was visibly upset.

"I'll check out the field house running track tomorrow after school," he told her.

3

Mike Gibbons enlisted in the Navy shortly after high school graduation. He could not afford college but decided to complete his military duty and further his education using the GI Bill. Wrestling in high school had served him well and helped preserve his fitness. After completion of boot camp in Great Lakes, Illinois, he finished the curriculum in the Shore Patrol School, also at Great Lakes. His tall stature; broad shoulders; thick, well-groomed blond hair; and blue eyes would make him a perfect poster boy for Navy recruiting. Mike's active duty orders sent him to a naval hospital in Virginia. While stationed there, he often went to the gym and worked out to preserve his strength and health. When not at the gym, he enjoyed an eight to ten-mile trek around his usual traffic pattern of city blocks or sometimes in the park a few blocks from where he lived.

During these runs, Mike rarely broke out in a heavy sweat, but today he could feel it. The jog, this time, seemed strenuous. Maybe it was the humidity making the run feel like drudgery. Some days, he flew like a horse on a racetrack, and some days, he felt like a donkey trudging up a hill. Today was a donkey day. The perspiration eased down his back and legs. His running shorts were damp. It was mid-May, with summer in full bloom.

A young woman happened to be sitting on a bench at the entrance to the park, with Mike running toward her. She was leaning forward, tying her shoelaces. They had passed each other a few times only recently. Mike stopped to say hello, and she responded, raising her head and brushing her light-brown hair back, while looking at him from the side of her face, smiling. Her body appeared lean and fit.

"I've seen you before. Do you come here often?"

"I'm new to this area, and I like it. I plan to come here often, but I have such a difficult time keeping these laces tied. The shoes are new, and the laces get loose on me." She pointed to her right foot.

"Can I show you how to tie 'em so they don't come undone? I had the same problem, and a saleslady at the shoe store showed me what to do."

"Sure. If you know how, I'd be grateful. I hate losing my stride, having to stop and retie them."

Mike knelt on one knee and started to lace the right shoe. They were the latest style of New Balance and obviously new. Looking up at her face, he said, "Oh, I'm sorry. My name is Mike."

"Hi. I'm Mary. And yes, in the short time I've been here, I've seen you using the park. You're a good runner." She cocked her head, and her hair fell in light-brown waves to one side. Her brown eyes crinkled when she smiled. "Been doing it long?"

"I ran through high school and never gave it up. I was on the wrestling team, which was demanding. Running was a must. Do you run marathons?"

"No, I'm just an exercise runner."

"Me too. Done. Laces secured."

"Hey, thanks. It was annoying to have to stop. Wanna join me? I'm fast!" Mary said, turning her head with a big smile as if she had been waiting to meet Mike for some time. "You may have a tough time keeping up."

Mike admired her attractive looks and body. "Let's go! At my age, I promise I'll do my best to keep up with you." He nodded, hoping he could fall behind to get a glance at her narrow backside.

Off they went, engaging in casual conversation along the way. Mary picked up the pace a little, and Mike kept the same stride, falling behind on purpose and just happening to look at her posterior. *That was thoughtful of her,* Mike thought. He took a peek, not a look, just a peek. Mike picked up the pace and caught up with Mary.

"Lived here long?" he asked.

"I just moved about a month ago. I used to live near Virginia Beach, but I hated the commute, so I now have a townhouse apartment on Front Street."

"I live on Front, also."

"What a coincidence."

When they finished, he walked her to her apartment building, which was on the way to his. The tree-lined street, perfectly laid out with apartments, townhouses, and a few single-family homes. The gardens appeared well-kept, making it a desirable place to live. Their conversation seemed pleasant and comfortable. Mike enjoyed the moment.

"Well, Mary, that was fun, and I'm glad to see you could keep up with me. I'm going out for beer and pizza in about an hour. Care to join me?"

"Yes, I would love to! I haven't anything to eat at my place. I'm still unpacking, so I need to go grocery shopping tomorrow." *I do have food, but I thought he'd never ask.*

"Give me a call when you're ready. I'll pick you up."

"Will do." She smiled at him while he gave her his phone number.

"And by the way, who kept up with whom?"

4

Mary called around five fifteen to tell Mike she was ready. He climbed into his VW Beetle and headed over to her apartment complex just a couple of blocks away.

Mary worked at the investment firm of Pollock, Barnes, and Jones, better known as PB&J, as an analyst and consultant in retirement funds. She had been living about eighteen miles east of her workplace, and the daily drive had become too expensive and fatiguing, even though the sun was always at her back going to and from work. The firm had employed her for about three years, and she liked the work she did. She had been employed as an intern during summer months at PB&J while in college, and the firm had offered her a full-time position on graduation. The pay was good, but as always, it could be better. She would usually jog after her workday.

Mary and Mike seemed comfortable with each other, and it was fun for Mike to get away from the Navy for an evening.

When he arrived at her apartment, she was outside. Mike got out and opened the car door for her. He returned to the driver's seat and said, "Any favorites?"

"The pizza place I like best is Napoli Pizza on Peterborough Parkway. It's not far from here. How about you? Any choices?"

Mike had a smirky smile. "That's okay, but I'd like to go to Napoli Pizza on Peterborough Parkway. Okay with you? It's not far from here.

I've been there before, but it's been a while. Besides, the ride will be perfect on such a great day."

Mary chuckled with a big smile, slowly shaking her head from side to side, realizing Mike had a sense of humor.

The day was ideal. The VW ran smoothly. He'd inherited it when his grandma had died two years ago, and he'd taken good care of it. He washed and waxed it once a month for protection from the sun and always enjoyed a cold beer after. The only drawback was, it didn't have a gas gauge. Radio? Yes. Gas gauge? No. There was a lever next to the gas pedal, which you applied with the toe of your shoe when the car started to sputter and slug along, signaling it wanted some gas. The lever, when activated by the toe of your foot, would open a one-gallon auxiliary tank, which allowed him to get to a gas station soon. Mike never let the tank get low. He filled it often, so it was generally full.

With the windows rolled down, he could smell the fruity aroma of Mary's freshly washed hair. *It's fun to be out and with her.*

The traffic seemed lighter than usual for this time of the day, so they arrived in about thirty minutes. He parked and went around, opening her door.

They entered Napoli Pizza. As they sat in a comfortable booth near the window, Mike knew the work crowd would arrive soon, and it would get crowded. The smell of garlic permeated the atmosphere, and after ordering two beers, they looked over the pizza menu.

"Any recommendations?" Mike asked.

"They're all good; some are just better than others. The margarita is simple, with tomatoes, cheese, and basil, but if you'd prefer some sausage or pepperoni, I'm game. Anything is fine."

"I see they'll do a half-n-half."

"You're right. I forgot to mention it."

"Do you like anchovies?"

"Sorry. I don't care for them at all," she replied, turning up her nose and showing her teeth.

"Then half-and-half it is. I love anchovies on pizza."

They had just finished half of their beer, and the server came to take their order. Mary wanted the margarita, and Mike the pepperoni with anchovies. They also ordered another beer when the server had time.

"So tell me," Mike asked, "Were you born and raised here?"

"No. Honolulu is my birthplace."

"Honolulu?" He said with an upward lilt to his voice. "What brought you here?"

Mary sat rubbing her fingernails against the red-and-white-checkered tablecloth. She tilted her head and smiled. "My father was in the Navy, so we traveled to several different ports of call. He transferred to Manila as base commander of Subic Bay when I was five; Alameda in Oakland, California, when I was ten; and then here when I was fifteen."

"That's a lot of moving. I suppose you just kept getting settled and then having to pull up roots to go somewhere else."

"You know it. My dad retired as an admiral and now and lives in Washington, DC, with my mom. All the moves were hard transitions because I had friends in school. I always hated to leave. Moving here was the most difficult because I started the tenth grade not knowing anyone. How about you? Tell me about yourself."

Mary sat quietly and waited for Mike to speak.

"Wow!" Mike sat shaking his head. "I wouldn't care to move around. You just settle in and have to up and run. And I know what you mean about friends. Did you adjust?"

"Yes, I did. As my dad always said, 'You have to flow with the go.'"

They both laughed, and Mike realized she was not only engaging and pleasant to look at, but it was also delightful to be with her.

"Now it's your turn," she prodded. "As I said, how about you? Where are you from?"

"Well," he hesitated, wondering if it was too early, given that they'd just met, to go into the details of his life so far. Many people already knew about Mike's origin, so it was comfortable for him to tell his story.

He decided, why not? So he began. "I grew up in a small town in southern Michigan near Ann Arbor. I never knew my parents. My mom died when I was four in a single-car auto accident because of a brain aneurysm. I never knew who my father was, as my mom chose to give me life with the help of a sperm donor."

Mary had a slight smile and a look of curiosity on her face as if to say, "really" and was about to speak when Mike continued.

"My grandparents took over when my mom died, and they raised me. My grandfather died when I was five. My grandma died just two years ago."

"What an incredible story! Have you ever done research to try to find your father?"

"No, I haven't, but I have always been curious about something."

"Yes, and that is?"

"I've been curious whether the doctor performing the insemination procedure had a cigarette after."

Mary laughed out loud. Tears came to her eyes she laughed so hard. So did Mike.

"That is hilarious."

Smiling, Mike took a sip of his beer—no, not a sip, a gulp.

"I have a copy of my birth certificate with my mother's name, and the space for my father's name reads, 'unknown.' I wonder if I resemble my father. Did he have blond hair and blue eyes like me? Was he tall or short, strong or muscular, fat or slim, pleasant or gruff? Did he like sports like me? Did he like women as I do? I not only haven't had the time to research, I never knew how to go about doing it. Besides, I have no idea if he's living or dead or where he is. It's a double-edged sword."

The server came with the second round of beer and said the pizza would be up shortly.

"Your story is the beginning of a book. It's intriguing. My English writing professor always said, 'there's a story in everything.' And so far, she is so right on! I'm sure you could get help with the research if you wanted. The library is always a good place to start. When I was in college, I used the librarians. I'm sure they'd direct you where you need to go to start. They can also show you where to go to find some answers."

Mike didn't react or return a comment, and the moment became quiet.

Mary looked at Mike with a smile. "Sorry. I don't mean to intrude on your life."

"No, no, Mary. Don't even think you are. Everyone I grew up with knew my background even before I did. I was fourteen when my grandma talked to me about it. I've always had the curiosity, but I always considered my dad as Daffy Duck the Donor. He was never a father to me. I never moved forward with it. What I might find out concerns me."

There was a silence as they both took a sip of beer. It left the moment open as to who would speak next.

"By the way, where'd you go to college?" Mike changed the subject.

"I graduated from William and Mary in Williamsburg, Virginia. I applied to other colleges and universities, but tuition is so steep I couldn't see doing it just to get a degree from who knows where. I did receive a small scholarship in economics, so I decided to use it there. No one so far has asked for my transcript. And, Mike, please don't refer to your father as 'Daffy Duck the Donor.'"

Mike reacted by closing his eyes and raising his eyebrows, making a facial expression as if to say, *well, what the hell do you want me to call him?*

The pizza came. "Wow! Look at those anchovies! It looks and smells delicious. Aren't you glad I had the idea to come here?"

Mike looked at Mary, who turned her head slightly as if to say, *Yeah, right.* However, she didn't say anything. She just flashed him a smile. Mike responded with the same expression.

"Keep those anchovies swimming on your side of the plate," she said. "I could never eat them. In fact, I don't care much for fish. Maybe crab, shrimp, or lobster, but not fish fish. I think it comes from my parents having fish all the time in Honolulu and Manila. We enjoyed a mixed cuisine once we were on the mainland."

Mary could not eat all of her side of the pizza, but Mike consumed all of his, as well as the one piece of Margarita Mary left on the tray.

"Delicious. Great suggestion! Great place! Great company!" Mike said.

Mary smiled, agreeing. They clinked their glasses; Mike paid the bill, and they left.

5

The weeks went by, with Mike getting closer to his release date. It was exciting to have met Mary. They ran about twice a week and always on weekends. They went for walks, movies, and spent the free time each had, together. He felt more than closeness to her but also realized he would be leaving soon. He knew he would miss her. August 11, his departure date, was not far away.

During Mike's days when he didn't run, he would spend time going off somewhere, sitting down, and listening to one of the recordings he had on his iPhone. He would listen to tapes about exercise, loneliness, curbing alcohol consumption, eating, sleeping, and other selections. He often thought of the murder at Chestnut and Grand. It was a tragic event, but the perpetrator had been caught and had been sentenced.

He felt a fondness for Mary and wondered if he could fall in love. *I can't*, he thought, pounding his fists on the ground. He wasn't ready for it. His thoughts turned to Mary. *But I like her. We are so compatible together. We will be friends and maybe see what happens later.* Putting his hands on his head, he thought harder. *I can't fall in love right now. I just can't. I have too much ahead of me. Love has to come later.*

The Fourth of July came. Mary and Mike went to the beach for the afternoon. They planned to return to his place, barbecue a couple of steaks, and consume a few drinks and a good Cabernet with the meal.

He liked scotch, but this time of the year, gin and tonics were the order of the day. He had all the ingredients.

The sky was clear and the sun penetrating. They brought plenty of sunscreen, a beach umbrella and a couple of beach chairs, and a cooler of bottled water and a few beers. Mike put a good amount of Coppertone on his arms, legs, and torso.

He was well built, and this was the first time Mary saw him with his shirt off. She always suspected he presented with a good-looking physique, but now, instead, she decided he was a hunk.

"Would you put some of this lotion on my back?" he asked.

"Sure, if you'll do the same for me."

"Gladly!" he said, nodding while raising his eyebrows and grinning.

Mary rubbed the Coppertone on his back, and his skin was smooth, tight, and well-muscled.

"I have to put some below the waistband of your suit, which is a vulnerable spot for sunburn."

"Go ahead."

Mary slid her hand under the band of his shorts and felt the firmness at the top of his buttocks. His dimples of Venus were prominent, and she lightly rubbed her fingers into and over them. She liked how they looked on well-muscled men.

Mike turned around. "Thank you. I liked it; felt good. I'm not into massages, but that was a good one." There was a look in their eyes, which confirmed a sudden connection.

"You have taken good care of yourself physically. Did you play any other sports?"

"No, just the wrestling team starting in the sixth grade. I learned a lot about self-defense, and I never have anyone messing with me. With the moves I know from my training on the mat, it would not be smart for someone to approach me with the wrong idea."

Mary gave the bottle to Mike for her back as she had already covered her front side. She wore a bikini, which tied with a small cord at each hip and on the back of the halter. *Not too bad.* Mike lathered her up first on the shoulders.

"Undo my halter at the neck and around my back so you can cover all of my back."

Mike pulled the cords as Mary held the top to her. Mike continued to rub in the Coppertone. He moved his hands to the left and right sides near her breasts. She didn't object. Going further down, he arrived at her waist on the backside.

"Do you want me to put some below your waistband like you did for me?"

"I did it for you; you can do it for me."

Mike squeezed the lotion in his hands and slowly slid them under the waistband of her bikini. His fingers drifted in the crevice between her buttocks. What a pleasant butt! *I'd better contain myself*, he thought. But the trouble was, he didn't want to. Finished, he secured her halter around her back and neck. They were in for a great afternoon.

6

"I'm glad we brought the umbrella."

"Yes. Getting sunburned is not fun. Even with the umbrella, we could still get reflection off the water, and you can still burn just the same. I don't need it, with having to go to work tomorrow."

"Me either. I go on sentry duty at six in the morning."

They sat together, Mary quietly reading and Mike listening to a CD. At one point while seated under the umbrella, Mike took his earphones off, and Mary asked, "Do you listen to music?"

"Sometimes, but I mostly enjoy meditation."

"Meditation! I've heard it can improve your life. It tends to help you become a contented person. I'm convinced I should try it. I just haven't taken the step."

Mike smiled. "I suppose you could say I'm contented. I guess it shows, but it's in the eye of the beholder. I've always been angry about my father, but more so about my mother's death. Somehow, I've always felt cheated in life by being parentless, although I cherish growing up with my grandma. I enjoy the recordings and try to listen to them ten to fifteen minutes every day. I've done it since high school."

Mary thought for a moment. "Like I said, I've never done anything like it. Maybe I should consider shaping up my life a little."

"I have enjoyed listening to my CDs, as I said. They were hard to get into at first. I couldn't understand where they were taking me. It

The Day Always Comes

was a journey I was not familiar with or even seeking. In the beginning, it seemed like torture." Looking at Mary, Mike continued. "You don't seem in bad shape, either physically or emotionally, but you alone have to be the judge. You have a good job; I have a feeling you're well respected by your firm and clients."

Mike went on to explain his interest and background in meditation. "I think it started with not knowing my parents. As I progressed in listening to the CDs, I became aware of a greater understanding of people. It took me away from the constant chatter. I was never a troublemaker in school, but I did get into some fights and arguments with my friends about my calling my grandma 'mom.' I was angry they stuck their nose into it. It was none of their business. I always felt lonely, although I frequently have heard voices in my head, and I hate it. Am I talking too much?" Mike smiled and Mary said, "No, not at all. I find it interesting, and I can almost visualize what you are saying. Please continue."

Mary sat still, sensing Mike hesitated, wanted to talk, and he opened up to her.

"The town I grew up in was so small I attended a four-room schoolhouse for grades one through eight, two in each room. There were eight students in my class. I always said when we graduated, they set up two card tables for our celebration. I went to the local high school with 625 students in four upper grades. My grandma made sure I behaved myself. She didn't put up with any nonsense. My grades in high school were good, and I was in the upper third of my class. The wrestling team was my life. I couldn't afford to go on to college, so I decided to join the Navy and planned to continue my education after my release from active duty on the GI Bill. When my grandma died two years ago, she left me with some money and the VW." Mike stopped, looked up and smiled.

Mary listened and smiled back in appreciation of how he was opening to her. "I guess I'm telling you this because you told me all about your early years of going from place to place. I've told others along the way, but you're the only one here who knows my whole story. The others only know pieces. I'm alone in life. I say that because I have no relatives."

"Thank you," Mary replied with a smile, a gesture of appreciation.

Once or twice they went into the ocean, and walking along the shore was refreshing. After about four hours, a couple of beers, chips, and water, they decided to go back to the apartment. Mary said she would fix a potato salad while Mike was the bartender for the gin and tonics and the chef to grill the steaks, which he had bought earlier. The traffic was not heavy. They were ahead of everyone heading back to the city, so they made it in a short time. Besides, Mike had a pleasant, entertaining thought in his mind.

"Let's leave the umbrella and chairs in the car. We can get them to your place when I take you home. I'll help you with them."

"Okay."

They went into Mike's apartment. The air-conditioning had been on, so the place felt comfortable.

"If you'd like to take a shower to get rid of the sea, sand, and sun lotion on your body, you're welcome to do so. I always hate the sticky, dirty feeling coming in from the beach."

"I think I will, but all I have to put on is my bikini and this short shirt."

Mike smiled, tilted his head, and raised the palm of his left hand.

"Not a problem. I have a long T-shirt if you want. My grandma gave it to me. It's a guy's nightgown. I never wear it. Navy men don't wear pajamas. They sleep in their skivvies. It's clean, never been worn, and would go down to your knees."

"Oh, that's great, I'll take you up on it.

They went into the bedroom, where Mike directed Mary to the bathroom for her shower.

"There's shampoo here if you want. It's generic, but it works for me."

"It'll be just fine."

Mike went to his dresser and pulled out the nightshirt. He put a large towel on the table in the bathroom, closed the door to the bedroom, and left for the kitchen.

He could hear the shower running and decided to get out the ingredients for the G&Ts and the potato salad. He took the charcoal and lighter out and readied it for the Weber grill but did not light it. Mary came out of the bedroom, draped in his long nightgown T-shirt. She looked beautiful and smelled feminine even though she had used Mike's soap and shampoo.

"Hey, you look great. It fits you perfectly!"

"I love it. I feel naked in it."

Mike loved her reaction and smiled, raising his eyebrows. He took his turn in the shower and put on clean running shorts and no T-shirt. They both kept on their flip-flops.

When he came back to the kitchen, Mary had taken the pre-cooked potatoes from the refrigerator, cut them into pieces, chopped the celery, onion, and a couple of radishes. Mike fixed each of them a gin and tonic. He handed it to her, smiled, clinked his glass with hers, and said, "Here's to you, and here's to me. What a fun afternoon it was meant to be. So here's to us!"

"I loved it too, Mike. Thank you."

Mike enjoyed the word *love*, and he had a rush through his body as he watched Mary sipping her gin and tonic. He could feel an attraction at this moment, something he had not experienced before. Her lips were a beautiful red, like raspberries fresh from the vine, and he wanted them lightly pressed to his. There was a quiet while they both sipped their drinks. The moment was very refreshing, and Mike felt a surge of warmth and electricity rush through his body. He looked down at her small frame and smiled with a devilish, intense eye contact.

They took a sip, continuing to look into each other's eyes without saying a word. Mike put his drink down, placed his arms around her waist, and pulled her gently close to him. Mary did not resist. She put her glass down next to his and placed her hands around Mike's triceps.

They slowly moved their faces toward each other, their lips coming together smoothly and softly in a warm embrace.

After a minute or less, Mike said, "Why don't we put the potato salad in the fridge and relax for a while."

Mary smiled. Without saying a word, she reached over, handed Mike the bowl, and opened the refridgeator door.

7

Mike liked to escape to various places just to be alone. He never told anyone where he was going or what he was doing but always took his iPhone with him. He had a clandestine manner about himself and no one asked or suspected his whereabouts. He would, most of the time, just sit and reflect on his life and his anger about not knowing his parents and events in the past. His mother, he accepted. His father, he did not. Besides, he felt Mary thought of him as contented. He was happy but often thought about himself genetically. *What's my ethnic background? What did my dad look like? Do I look like him? Was he athletic? Educated?* With his curiosity at a high point, he headed back to his apartment.

He was driving down High Street when he saw the library on the corner he was approaching. He remembered the night at Napoli Pizza, how Mary had wondered if he'd ever thought of finding his father. He had asked himself that same question many times, but he'd never expressed it. He had always been curious, and as the years had gone by, he had become more interested. *Maybe I should seriously start to look into it*, he thought. *Where would I begin?* he wondered. As he'd said to Mary, "My father is just a donor in my book." As Mary had suggested, the library would be as good a place to start as any; at the least the librarian would be able to point him in the right direction. He wondered for a moment if it was time.

Out of curiosity, he parked, entered, and went inside to the information desk.

"Hello. May I help you?" The woman behind the desk was young and attractive. She greeted Mike with a smile.

"I'm looking for my father. I don't know where to begin."

The librarian looked at Mike quizzically. "Did he come into the building with you?"

"No, no. Oh, I'm sorry. I don't mean to confuse you," Mike smiled, understanding what he'd said and why she looked confused. "I might as well tell you straight on. My mother birthed me from a sperm donor. I don't know who he is, but I am interested in finding out about him. Would it be difficult to do?"

The librarian put her head back, smiled, and said, "I thought your father was somewhere around here in the building. Now I understand what you mean. Yes, it is possible to find the donor, but also, it could be difficult, and it might even be impossible." The librarian smiled and extended her hand. "My name is Joan Stevens, and I'm glad to help you."

"Thank you." Smiling and extending his hand in return, he said, "I'm Mike Gibbons. This is my first inquiry. I have never done any research before, so I don't have a clue how to start or what to do."

"Not a problem, Mike. I've worked with people who have had similar questions, and I'm here and glad to help you. Let me ask you a few questions."

Joan took out a form and asked Mike where he was born; his date of birth; and details about his childhood, including where he'd lived, what education he'd received, and his grandparents' surnames and given names. After writing the information down and being satisfied with Mike's answers, Joan rose from her desk.

"Let's start with the statistics section over here," she said, pointing toward the area across from her. "We can begin with the year of your birth and location where you lived. First, however, I must tell you to assume nothing. Expect nothing. You may find nothing."

Mike listened with a look of curiosity.

"Your search could be long and complicated. Just the same, it could be quick and easy. It will also depend on the donor's wish, if he had any. It sounds as if you have no information with which to start."

"Correct, and that's why I came here. The young woman I'm dating told me to make the library my first stop to help me get started."

"Good advice. We have inquiries a couple of times a year, so we put together a guide for anyone looking for their parents, whether it's the mother or the father, and even siblings. If the donor gave more than one sample, you could have some half brothers and half sisters."

"Oh, wow. I never thought of that. I guess I've discovered some new information already." Mike gave a smile and a look of acceptance.

"I would suggest you check out this guide, take it home, and read through what you can. It will give you information as to where to find further material. It also guides you to resources on the Internet. It's rather a lengthy read, so jot down any questions you might have as they come to you, along with the page number. After you read and gain all the information you want right now, come back and I can help you with wherever you want to continue next. I'm glad to assist you when you need it." Joan looked at Mike and took in the serious expression that had crossed his face. "I hope this isn't too much information at this time?" she asked gently.

"No, no, no. I guess it's where you have to start. I had no idea. And thanks so much. I think this will keep me busy for a while and out of trouble. Wish me luck."

"Okay. I wish you luck. I hope you find what you're looking for, and I also hope this will be a pleasant journey."

They smiled and shook hands. Mike continued to the checkout desk.

He left the library and headed home. It was late afternoon. He stopped at a local bar called the Watering Hole to have a cold one before dinner. He celebrated, as he had now officially begun the search and the adventure of finding his father. He'd often felt the desire but had never done the research. He remembered, from one of his tapes, an Irish proverb: "The longest journey begins with a single step." He had just taken the first step, and, he decided, however many detours, dead ends, or roadblocks he faced, he would accept the results.

The drive to the apartment was uplifting, with a feeling of excitement. The beer was just what he'd needed. Mike had never thought he would actually start such an inquiry. At this point, all he wanted to know about his father was his height, hair color, and other physical characteristics. He had no intention of meeting him. He didn't care if he was living or dead. He knew who his mother was, as his grandmother had told him stories and showed him pictures of her. He could tell she loved her daughter. He knew her sudden death because of a brain aneurysm had been a tragic loss, and he was aware of the tragedy of a parent losing a child. Mike wondered if his early child behavior had had anything to do with her headaches. He wondered. Yes, he wondered. He wondered about a lot of events in his past.

He fixed a dish of pasta, opened another brew, and sat down to watch the news and thumb through the wealth of material Joan had given him.

8

The day began rainy and humid. Mike was on duty until two. The sky cleared, making the humidity even greater. He hurried home to check the mail, have a bite to eat, and get ready to go out to buy some groceries, but first and foremost, he checked his voicemail. There was a message from Mary, saying she could meet him after work.

"I'd love to meet you," her message said. "I should finish around four, so I'll give you a call when I am ready. If it doesn't work, give me a jingle."

Mike decided her suggestion would work, so he did not call Mary back and sat down for a quick review of the information Joan had given him the day before. He wanted to sound like he knew what he was talking about when he met Mary.

The phone rang about four thirty. She said the day at the office had been busy and strenuous, and she needed a good workout. They'd talk about it when they met. Mike walked to her apartment building. They greeted each other with a big hug and a kiss, and then they started off.

"Oh, what a day," she told him. "Three new clients, all looking for help entering their retirement. Three in one day is too much for me."

Their pace continued, and they talked without effort.

"I'm sure you handled it," he said.

"So what's your news? How was your day?"

"Well, it started yesterday. I decided to do some research and look for the man responsible for fertilizing my mother's egg and giving me life."

Mary stopped. She looked at Mike with a quizzical smile and approving nod. "Unreal! I am so happy for you. Tell me all about what you're going to do."

The run continued at a slightly slower pace because of the humidity. Mary appeared pleased, and Mike was excited to tell her all about it.

"I picked up a quote in my material by Trell. I don't know who the hell he is or where he tends bar, but I've decided it's true what he said; 'It takes more than just a donor to be a father.'"

Mary gave Mike a pat on the butt. "I am so happy for you. It's going to be exciting."

"I was out yesterday afternoon and happened to drive by the downtown library. I remembered what you said the night we went to Napoli, asking me if I ever had wanted to do a search. I said he was just a donor in my book, but I decided there's more to it. Come on. Let's run. Burger and fries after?"

"Sounds great! Where are you planning on going?"

"How 'bout Southwick on Queen Street?"

"I haven't been there for some time. I like the place, so you're on!" Mary sounded excited, and they picked up the pace a little more.

"Good. I'll pick you up after we shower and change. Wanna come to my place to clean up?"

Mary looked at Mike with a smirk on her face. "You rascal! I know what you'd rather do than have a burger and fries. But if you're good to me tonight, well, maybe we can work something out."

"In advance, I'll be good to you.

9

The next morning, Mike reported to the internal medicine clinic at the Naval Hospital to have his departure physical. The doctor discovered he had a heart murmur. He encouraged Mike to stay on active duty and have it evaluated.

"I can't. I'm going to a University in Tampa, Florida, to study criminology, and everything is all set. Am I required to stay?"

"Well, it isn't serious, and you are not required to stay," the doctor continued. "But you should be aware it could develop into atrial fibrillation. If you don't wish to stay, it's your choice. But you should see a cardiologist regularly to have a checkup." The doctor continued, "Did either of your parents ever talk about an irregular heartbeat? Or did they have a diagnosis of a-fib?"

"I never heard the term until right now."

With the physical finished and the only finding the murmur, Mike went on his way, intent on keeping his meeting with Mary during her lunch hour. All the while, he thought about the murmur. How could this be? *I'm very active; I'm lean; and, most of all, I'm young.*

He wondered if it was a family abnormality he'd received from one of his parents. The diagnosis made him think even more about how he wanted to find his donor father. He met Mary and didn't say anything about the physical findings.

"I'll let you know what time we can meet today," Mary said. "It should be around four, but I'll call and leave you a message."

After lunch, he had some time and decided to go outside and walk. It was a beautiful day. He wanted to think, and he wanted to meet Mary after she was through with work. About a half hour later, at twelve fifty-five he went to the first-floor office of Enlisted Administrative Separations (ADSEP) to review and sign his release documents. Mike completed the necessary paperwork in preparation for his discharge and headed home.

॰॰

At four o'clock, Mike and Mary were at the park. Mike started and took off.

"Better get hopping. I'm already ahead of you," he called out.

"Settle down, sailor! I'll be ahead of you before you know it!" Mary picked up her pace and was soon matching Mike's pace alongside him.

"Signed my departure papers today. It looks like they're gonna get rid of me."

"Their loss is the world's gain."

"I think your compliment suggests we should go out. I have more to tell you."

"Gee, you sure like to go out to eat a lot."

"I do," Mike replied. "I have two fetishes in life—running and eating out. Well, maybe three."

They both looked at each other with a knowing smile.

"Where to?" Mary asked.

"Anywhere you want to go. Your choice. McDonald's, Burger King, a movie, How about Subway, or just a walk."

Chuckling, Mary replied, "Okay. Let me think. I'll let you know when you pick me up."

Mike smiled back.

He left Mary at her doorstep and went to his place to clean up.

10

It was six. Mary was ready and looked gorgeous. She smelled good, too. They took off in the VW.

"Where to, my lady?"

"How about Castellano's?"

"Sounds better than my suggestions. Maybe the patio will be available."

Parking was easy, the patio was available, and the host seated them right away. Mary thought a margarita sounded delicious. Mike decided to have a beer. The drinks came. They told the server they were in no hurry and would order a second round before they ordered.

"As you wish," the server said. "If you change your mind, just flag me down."

They toasted each other, and Mary said, "I can't believe we have only a week left. Why didn't we meet earlier?"

"God! I don't know, but I wish we had," Mike replied. "I had my exit physical today." He hesitated and said slowly, "I have a heart murmur."

"What?" She was taken aback, and her voice had an incredulous tone. "How could you have a heart murmur with all the cardio exercise you do?"

"Doesn't matter, the doctor said. The EKG confirmed it. You can't cheat it. He told me I could have inherited it from one of my parents."

"Did you say anything to him about your father?"

"No." Mike squinted with a serious look. "If I don't know who my father is, how can I give him any information about my health?"

"Mike, you don't understand the importance of him knowing."

"So what would he find out? I don't know my father, so I don't even know. And besides, what am I supposed to say? I have no idea whether the murmur came from, my mother or Daffy Duck." Mike laughed, more of a chuckle, but it was without humor. The anger made his eyes narrow and his voice tight.

"Hey!" Mary placed her open palm flat on the table. "This is serious, Mike. Don't treat it so lightly. It isn't funny. You could be the son of a business executive, a wealthy man, or maybe it was just a college student who needed the money."

"Yeah, and he could have been a druggie, a bum, a panhandler."

Mary slapped her hand on the table again, pursed her lips, raised her voice and looked pointedly, serious-faced, and impatiently at Mike. "Damn, Mike! You get so upset sometimes. You can't think in such negative terms. So what if he was a bum, a panhandler, or just an ordinary guy. He was, or is, a human being, and he is still your father. You don't even know if he's alive."

"Boy, you've calmed down a lot since I first met you." Mike tried to make the scene calmer and gritted his teeth. "I want to be open to anything and everything. I am not humorous about it. Like the librarian said, 'Take nothing for granted.' That's precisely the attitude I intend to use."

Mary shook her head. "I'm sorry," she said and hesitated. "I just want you to take this seriously and be methodical about it. It is what it is! Maybe my days at William and Mary are showing."

"You don't have to apologize. I have some ideas, and I plan to start my research as soon as I arrive in Florida."

The mood became quiet. Both smiled at each other, and Mike gave the server a wave of the hand. "Another round if you would please," he said.

The server came with the drinks, and they ordered. They continued to sit in the afternoon warmth and just have a pleasant conversation. The mood had calmed down.

Just then, a gentleman and a lady approached Mike and Mary's table. The man was Admiral Mike Gibbons, with whom Mike coincidentally shared a name, and the woman, Mike would soon learn, was the admiral's wife. Upon first arriving at the Naval Hospital, Mike had been surprised to learn he shared a first and last name with the admiral, though the two had different middle names.

"Mike," the admiral said. "Good to see you out and about."

Mike immediately started to get up from his seat.

"No, no, no. Please stay seated. Thank you for your courtesy," the admiral said.

Mike was halfway up, so he continued to stand. The admiral put out his hand to shake with Mike.

"Good evening, sir, or is it still afternoon? It's good to see you, and, if I may say respectfully, in civilian clothes."

Admiral Gibbons chuckled. "Yes, I don't go around in my uniform all the time. Meet my wife, Lorraine."

"How do you do, ma'am. It's a pleasure, and I'd like you to meet my friend, Mary," he said, directing his open palm toward her. Mike returned to his seated position.

With introductions completed, the admiral said, "How's everything going?"

"Well, sir, I had my exit physical today. My discharge is next Tuesday, the eleventh."

"What? You're not making the Navy a career?' the admiral said with a smile and continued. "What's on your plate for the future?"

"I'm accepted at a university in Tampa, Florida. I plan to study criminology."

"That's great, Mike!" Lorraine said. "Will you be using the GI Bill?"

"Yes, ma'am. I couldn't afford college after high school, so I joined the Navy, and this is working out exactly as I had planned. Also, I have work to do on my genealogy. I started researching it recently and found it fascinating, so I'm going to continue exploring it."

"Well, Mike, come to my office on the eleventh. I'd love to see you off. I'll escort you to the front door."

Mike gave a smile and a nod of the head. He was definitely pleased.

While Mike and the admiral continued to chat, Mary and Lorraine engaged in conversation.

"Well, thank you, sir," Mike finally said. "I will plan to see you on the eleventh."

The two shook hands again, and Mary said, "It was delightful meeting you both."

The admiral and his wife left for their table.

"Wow, how sweet of him to stop,"

"I know, but I won't say it was sweet," Mike smiled, sending a message. "Guys only use the word sweet when speaking of candy. I would use the word kind or considerate. I see him every morning as he enters the base. He always says, 'Mornin', Mike.'"

"I think it's wonderful and exciting you've decided to continue searching for your father," Mary said with a big smile. "I also apologize for getting upset." He sat back and sighed. "It'll be an interesting adjustment not being on the base," he mused. "Suppose I'll have the search for Daffy Duck to distract me though."

Mike laughed, and Mary pursed her lips, shook her head, and smiled. Mike took in a deep breath. "Okay. I won't. Can I just call him Sam?"

"You are such a shit sometimes."

Both of them laughed, and the mood became calm.

The evening had a warm breeze. The sunset was beautiful. The food was excellent. The conversation was light compared to what it had been when they'd first arrived. Mike knew he would miss Mary. She had been a good and fun companion for the short time he had known her. He sensed she would be a loss to him in his life's journey. He looked at Mary, smiled, and thought, *Yes, I could fall in love.*

11

The week went by quickly. Besides being on duty at the main gate, Mike spent time going through his belongings and deciding what he would take with him. He hadn't bought much during his tour of duty; just the same, he wondered how he'd accumulated so much. There was one item he'd brought with him and wanted to keep out of sight—out of mind. He kept it in a small, metal box with a lock. If anyone were to ask about it, he was prepared to say it contained some mementos from his mother. No one had ever seen what was in the box. It was locked, and he kept the key in a small plastic bag in a side pocket of his shaving kit.

A few boxes from the local liquor store would be enough. Mike and Mary spent time together jogging almost every day, and she helped him pack and sort. Mary took on the task of going through magazines. Mike loved monthly publications like *Men's Health*, *Men's Fitness*, *Muscle Development*, and so on. He respected his body and thought others should do the same with themselves. "It's the only body you have," he always said. Mike had learned this concept from his high school coach, his self-hypnosis, and meditation sessions. He tried to do them every day, taking twenty to thirty minutes to relax and to create a spellbinding experience. He practically had the CDs memorized. They helped him understand who he was, what he was, and where he was going.

"Wow! You sure like these men's magazines," Mary said, breaking into his thoughts.

"Well, women like *theirs*," he replied, stressing *theirs*. "What's wrong with men being interested in stuff about exercise and diet? Why do women always have to question men about what they like? Just because a guy is not doing what a woman wants, then it's …" Mike stopped.

Mary was looking at him, her mouth dropped open. She shook her head and said quietly, "What are you so worked up about? Gosh, I just asked a question, and you got all agitated."

The mood became quiet, and Mike became aware of his anger.

"I'm sorry. Sometimes I just get tired of certain things, especially questions." Mike continued, "What people don't realize is, they will take their body to the grave with them. Stay well, stay fit, work out, and work hard. All this and you will be a good-looking corpse. Besides, I have no interest in *Oprah*, *Vogue*, or *Ladies' Home Journal*. You know what I mean? And I am sorry for the outburst."

Mary sat quietly, wondering what it was that made him so upset. She had observed his outbursts before.

But now it was time for dinner. Mike had bought a couple of steaks for the Weber. He loved to cook out, and Mary enjoyed being there fixing a salad or side dish to complement the evening as she had done in the past. They both loved to eat, and run, and eat.

Mike went to his "sin locker," as he referred to his liquor supply, and took out the gin, tonic water, and a fresh lime from the refrigerator. It was time for a G&T. As he prepared the drinks, Mary cleaned the mushrooms to sauté and decided to steam the fingerling potatoes. Mike was a meat and potatoes guy, but not as an everyday menu.

"Here ya go," he said as he gave Mary the G&T. "Here's to the happy times we shared. I will miss this and, most of all, you."

"Thank you, Mike, and I will miss everything about our times together as well. I will not forget them."

The first round of drinks finished, Mike said, "Instead of another, why don't we go and relax for a while?"

Mary knew exactly what he meant. "Let's not tonight. I'm enjoying this time together."

Mike gave Mary a look of disappointment.

"I'll tell you what," Mary continued. "Why don't I bring my clothes tomorrow after work for Thursday morning? You're not planning to leave until Thursday, so we could have a farewell tomorrow night together. I'll clean up in the morning and leave from here."

"Well, sounds good. I like your idea."

Mike took the charcoal out to the grill and got it started. The steaks would take only eight to ten minutes, so everything else should be ready when they were done. He took out a bottle of Turley red, and they enjoyed a special meal together.

He took Mary home and returned to prepare for the next day.

12

Before Mike went to bed, he made sure his white summer uniform was clean, pressed, and necktie perfect. He shined his shoes and made sure his lid, the sailor's hat, was without threads. Tomorrow was Tuesday, August 11. He looked forward to his release from active duty by the admiral. Not everyone had this privilege. Meeting him was a high spot in his tour of duty. He asked Mike to come to his office at 1100 hours. Mike had everything prepared and ready.

The alarm sounded at six. He opened his eyes and said, "This is my discharge day. Today is the day."

The day always comes, he thought.

He sat up, put his headphones on, and listened to his meditation on "goal and shine." It took all of fifteen minutes. When finished, he got up, put on the coffee, and went to shave, shower, and get ready. Each time he opened his shaving kit, he put his hand on "the key." Clutching it, he pursed his lips, slowly moved his head from side to side, and said, "I'm sorry."

He did not put on his uniform right away but climbed into a pair of shorts and a T-shirt. He sat down with his coffee outside on the balcony and opened the morning paper. After reading all the news he didn't want to know about, he went to the cupboard, poured a bowl of shredded wheat'n bran with soy milk, and sat down to eat.

The Day Always Comes

It was now nine fifteen, and he thought he'd dress and head over to the hospital to complete his discharge. But first, he went out to his car and placed a clean, white sheet over the seat. At nine forty-five, he came out, started the car and drove toward the hospital. He parked in the correct parking space, went inside, and walked to the yeoman's office to sign and receive his DD 214 discharge papers. The Office of Financial Operations (FMO), where he would pick up his final pay and savings, was right down the hall. He finished all the paperwork and procedures and headed to the office of the commanding officer, Admiral Michael A. Gibbons. The only difference between their names was he was Michael J. Gibbons.

While walking through the checkout procedures, he thought of his mother, grandmother, and grandfather and, yes, his father. How he would have loved to have had his family there to see him discharged. No one was there, just Mike and the admiral. It seemed strange to see his name on the door, "Admiral Michael A. Gibbons, Commanding Officer." *Could Admiral Gibbons be my father?* He thought. Of course, he realized that was impossible, and he was never quite sure where the question, which arose in him from time to time around the admiral, came from. Even though they had the same name, there was no likeness. Besides, he had his mother's surname. He would not have his father's name, as he didn't know who his father was. Their shared name was just a coincidence.

Admiral Gibbons congratulated Mike and thanked him for his service to his country in the United States Navy.

After a few minutes of conversation, the admiral escorted him to the entrance of the hospital and saluted saying, "All the best Mike."

Mike returned the salute, thanked the admiral, shook hands with him, and departed.

Mike went to his car, and when he approached the main gate exit, four men and two women stood at attention and saluted him. He returned the greeting with a great big smile on his face.

"Have a pleasant life, Admiral Gibbons," one of them said with a big smile.

"Thank you. It was a privilege to work with all of you," Mike said. "And did anyone tell you, you're all bunch of clowns?"

Mike returned to the apartment and changed into his civilian clothes. It was noon. He went to the local Subway to grab a sandwich. He often did this because, as a guy, he would not always have food available at home. Besides, it was difficult to cook for one all the time. He enjoyed eating out, and since he knew he would be leaving soon, he cut back on having food around and in the refrigerator. Since meeting Mary, he'd found there was more food in the refrigerator than there had been previously, so he stopped going to the grocery store.

He called the property owner and discussed how he would leave the key. Because he had done such a good job of caring for the place, he had received his security deposit refunded to him a few days ago. He had immediately put it in his savings account.

"Boxes, boxes, stuff, clothes, duffel bag, shoes. How am I going to get all this crap in my VW?" Mike said aloud. He had to get ready for the morning, but more importantly, he wanted to get the place ready for a final evening with Mary. He didn't pack the car right away. He'd do it in the morning.

The phone rang. It was Mary.

"Mike, how'd it all go today?"

"Great! Everything went like clockwork. No hitches, which is not the usual Navy way."

"It always went as planned when my dad was on active duty."

"Oh yeah! But he was an admiral. I'm only third-class."

"Well, the reason I'm calling is, I'm going to be late tonight." She sounded hesitant because she knew what they had planned for the evening and didn't want to upset him.

Mike slumped, letting his chin bounce toward his chest; pursed his lips; took in a long, deep breath; and immediately took on a look of disappointment. He was so ready to enjoy a quiet sundown with a couple of G&Ts, some R & R, and a good dinner from the Weber.

"So? What's up?" He tried not to let the frustration show in his voice. His sigh, probably heard through the phone, set the tone.

"I hear that anger in your voice again." Mary paused, and there was silence from both of them. "We have a wealthy client coming in around five o'clock," she finally said. "The powers at PB&J want me to be there, as I have all the current data on retirement funds."

"Oh, how great! They need *you* to tell *them* what's going on in the retirement business. I suppose they'll give themselves a raise at the end of the year. All you'll get is a little pat on your butt. Then they'll give themselves a little pat on the palm of their hands, in the form of money." Mike was clearly angry—displaying an anger marked with frustration and disappointment.

"I know," Mary replied. "Don't get all overhyped again! It always seems so easy for you to do. Besides, that's not the way it works. I have to do this. It's my job. Didn't you have to do some extras when you were on active duty?"

"Right! I forgot. But I'm no longer on active duty. Thanks for telling me that."

"Don't be so sarcastic! Here we have such a wonderful time together, and I know it's our last night. I was looking forward to it as much as you. I'll get there as soon as I can, and I'll call just as I'm leaving."

"Good! I'll meet you at the door. We'll start with dessert."

"Mike, just chill it. I'll be there. I'll call. Please don't be upset for our last night together."

"I know. I'm sorry. We've never had a quarrel or an unkind word to each other, just my flipping anger, except when I refer to my dad as Daffy Duck."

"Oh! Here we go." She continued with some arrogance in her voice, "I'll be there, and I didn't know your surname was Duck."

"Smart-ass! Get here when you can. I'll be waiting."

They hung up.

Mike went on his way, trying to figure out what to do until she arrived. He slammed his fist on the table and gritted his teeth. He was too frustrated emotionally to settle down.

13

Time ran short. It was now eight forty-five, and Mike had not heard from Mary. He decided to go out for a beer. He called Mary's office phone and left a message: "Hey Mary, it's almost nine o'clock, and I'm hungry. Let's forget about tonight. I'll plan to pick you up at seven tomorrow morning. We'll go to the Craven Inn, have a good breakfast, and say good-bye there. Tonight would have been an enjoyable evening, but I guess it was not to be. If you can't make it because of a last-minute wealthy client, give me a call and leave a message. Now, isn't that sarcastic? See you in the morning."

Mike hung up, took his keys off the hook, and walked to his car. All the way to Edgar's Beer and Burgers, he fumed over the evening's change of plans. *I couldn't, nor would I want to, marry someone with whom plans changed because of a career,* he thought. *But then again, what about the job I want?* he asked himself.

Entering Edgar's, he saw a couple of his coworkers he had been on duty with at the main gate and, oh no, Tom and his talk, talk, talk girlfriend. She never shut up. Mike quickly scanned the bar. It was crowded; he had no way to go but forward. And when he looked up again, Tom had caught his eye. They had seen him. There was no escape.

"Hey, you guys. What's up?" he said, raising his left hand and trying to be cordial as he greeted Tom and Sue.

"Oh, you civilians. You always pop in when it's time to put in an order. We just got here about ten minutes ago. Join us. I'll buy you a beer," Tom said.

"Hey, thanks! I was hoping to have my girlfriend, Mary, with me, but she had to work late, so I'm glad to run into you. I need to get my mind off the disappointment," Mike lied. He wanted to be alone.

"I suppose you had a fun evening planned if know you what I mean," Sue said. "I know the last night of my tour of duty will be a good time. I always thought I would plan a trip to nowhere, but somewhere, just to get away from it all. I still have two years left, and I plan to spend them here. My mom always said, plan your life ahead. Make goals for yourself. I'm starting to do that ..." And she went on and on, blah, blah, blah.

Mike tuned her out and eventually interrupted, "Oh, you know me, huh? Well, I did have, or better yet, we had a fun evening planned. G&Ts, steaks on the grill, potato salad, and just a fun night together before I ship out tomorrow morning." *Doesn't this woman ever shut up?*

Tom and Sue smiled, and Mike raised his eyebrows with a wide-mouthed smile.

"You rascal. I envy you now, being able to go on your own," Tom said. "Still planning to go to the university near Tampa to study criminal behavior?"

"Criminology, Mr. Tom. Criminology,"

The server came. Mike ordered a beer and an Edgar House burger with fries.

"Boy, you'll sleep well on that one," Sue said starting in again. "Maybe it's good Mary isn't staying all night. But then again, you would be able to work off the calories ..." Sue said with a smile and then continued to ramble on and on.

But Mike cut her off again. "Now, who said she was going to stay with me? She's going to her place, and I'm going to mine. We're meeting in the morning and going to breakfast. You know I'm a clean-cut guy," he said with a smirk on his face.

"Yeah, right," Tom replied.

Mike started talking quickly so as not to give Sue the floor again. "As soon as I get to the university, I have to look for a place to live. Then I need to start a search for my family's history."

Mike planned to research his genealogy and had visited the library to return the material he'd checked out. He thought the librarian was cute, but she wasn't there when he dropped the material off. As passionate as Mike felt about his past, he didn't want to go into details, so he didn't mention his plans. At this point, there was no need for Tom and Sue to know.

The beer arrived, followed by the burger and fries about five minutes later. Mike devoured it, as he was hungry, hungry, hungry. He was glad he had gone to Edgar's, where so many of his Navy friends hung out. It was nine twenty. He finished, said good-bye to Sue and Tom, went out to the parking lot, and returned to his car. He had left his iPhone in the glove box and there was a message. He listened to Mary's voicemail: "Mike, I'm so sorry we couldn't be together this evening on your, or I should say, *our* last night together. Yes, I'll plan on breakfast in the morning and will be ready at seven. Again, I'm so sorry."

Mike turned the phone off without answering the message. *Maybe a good night's sleep will dissolve my feelings of disappointment.* Thinking of the evening with Tom and Sue, he thought, *I'm sure glad I don't date Sue. She would drive me nuts with her constant talking, talking, talking. But I've met some guys who do the same thing. I wouldn't date them either.*

Mike smiled and crawled into bed.

14

"I'm sorry I couldn't make it last night," Mary said as Mike opened the door for her. It was seven o'clock sharp, and she was ready.

"I'm sorry, too. It upset me, but a good night's sleep usually melts feelings away. I say, let it go. Sleep has always worked for me."

They started off to the Craven Inn, and Mike felt much better but would not forget.

"I know, Mike. It's been so fun getting to know you, and I've appreciated your kind heart, your warmth, our runs together; the pizzas, burgers, and fries; and especially you telling me about your family experience. I hope you will continue to chase the information you found in the book from the library and find what you're looking for. I hope you'll keep me up to date and we can meet again. I promise I won't screw up the night." Smiling, she said, "And I looked forward to it too."

Mike turned to Mary and smiled. He nodded his head. It was a forgiving smile. He realized that this was what one had to do in life sometimes, even when it wasn't what you wanted. He'd had moments like that before.

Mike said firmly, "I have a feeling you rehearsed your personal love letter in your mind during the night. Thank you so much, and I feel the same way. I know we did enjoy our time together. And if I wasn't in college, I think we could get something going about a permanent relationship."

Mary looked over at Mike, smiled, and put her hand on his on the steering wheel. "Mike, I am truly sorry."

They both knew and understood without saying a word.

They arrived at the Craven Inn about ten minutes later. Mike opened the door for Mary, and she put her arms around him and gave him a soft kiss on the cheek. "I will miss you. I think you know that."

Mike just smiled and put his arm out for her to take. "Well, parting is such sweet sorrow, but we'll be in touch. I won't forget you," Mike said as he closed the door.

They went inside.

The Craven was its usual busy morning. Many business people came there for breakfast. They were seated at a window table. The waiter came with a coffee pot in his hand.

"Good morning. Coffee for the two of you?"

"Mary?" Mike said.

"Oh yes, please," she replied.

"Thank you," Mike said, putting his cup closer to the waiter.

"Any cream or sugar?"

"Thanks. Neither of us uses it. We're on a diet," Mike replied.

Mary smiled because she knew they were both in great shape. They never used sugar in anything, and if either used cream, it was always fat-free. She now felt Mike was getting out of his moody shell.

"I think I'll miss your sense of humor. You pick up on words so fast and can make the moment funny."

Mike just sat and smiled back. "I've always been like that. I guess I get it from my father," Mike replied.

"See what I mean," Mary replied as they clinked their coffee cups together.

The waiter returned, asking if they were ready to order. They were, and Mary ordered the Craven Omelet. Mike decided on the eggs Benedict. "Thank you. It shouldn't take too long," the waiter replied.

"So now give me a rundown or timeline. What are your plans for today? I want to keep track of your every move while on the road."

Mike looked at Mary and thought, *We're not married, but there is the, where are you going, where will you be, what time will you get there?* Mike just smiled and let it pass.

"I plan to go back, load the car. In fact, I don't have as much as I thought. My duffel bag takes up most of the room, but it fits in the backseat. I plan to stop every hour and a half to fill up. I don't want to run out on the open highway. I usually can go for about three hours on a tank, so I have it all planned."

The conversation continued with some laughs about what they had done together since they'd met in June. The food arrived, along with a refill of coffee.

"Oh, this is delicious," Mary said. "I haven't been out for breakfast in a while.

"This is a real treat," Mike responded. "It sure beats the cafeteria's 'shit on a shingle' French toast or corned beef and eggs. I usually just grabbed a coffee and a bagel at the Gedunk."

The chitchat became quiet after they'd discussed what a beautiful day it was to be traveling south.

"I hope it isn't too hot in Florida. I've never been there this time of the year. Well, for that matter, I've never been there."

They both laughed.

"It will be an adventure. I've always wanted to travel to unknown places. As I have said to you before, I love the night, the quiet, and the sky littered with stars. It's wonderful to sit in meditation looking into space. It makes me think of my mom and dad, my grandma and grandpa, and where they are."

"Mike, you have a wonderful world of discovery ahead. Take it slowly and organize yourself. I'm sure it will all work out for you. Someday, I hope you will find your answer through meditation, and you will tell me all about it."

"I will. I promise. I've really weathered a rocky storm in my life, but I have received the gift of meditation and I think it is getting me through it. I've learned how to be more patient with myself and others. I have found a far-reaching sense of peace."

Mary didn't respond, only smiled, and looked at Mike with a proud expression.

The breakfast over, they walked to the car in the parking lot. Mike looked at the VW and turned to Mary. "I think first on my list of items to do when I get to Florida is to look into a new car. This one has served me well, but there always comes a time. The day always comes."

"You say that a lot. I believe it's your mantra. I think you deserve a new car and please get a gas gauge with it." Mary started to cry. "You've been a great friend."

"And you also." They embraced, and Mike continued. "I have to go now. I want to make it at least halfway before nightfall." There was a pause and stare. "Good-bye."

Mike turned to the car. He opened the door for Mary, she got in, and he drove her back to the apartment. He looked over at her. She did not look at him. He got out and went over to her door. She was crying. Getting out, they embraced, and he walked with her to the door of the building.

Mike put his hands on her chin and kissed her gently, tasting a salty drop of her tears, and she returned the kiss.

He walked back to the car, got in, and started the engine.

Mike looked at Mary; she was at the door crying, and he waved his left hand with a big smile. She waved her left hand and returned the smile. He went the few blocks to his apartment. Everything he was taking was ready, and he loaded it into his car.

He left the apartment keys on the table inside the door, as agreed with the landlord, got in the car, and drove off. It was nine fifteen.

15

Mike drove the distance to Tampa in one leg, stopping for gas every three hundred miles. He arrived on the outskirts of town around ten thirty. He saw the lights of a Comfort Inn with an IHOP next door.

He settled in, even though he had no reservation. After a good night's sleep, Mike sent off an e-mail to Mary:

> *Hey, Mary,*
>
> *I made it. The trip wasn't difficult, just long. I stopped to fuel up, and I never ran out of gas, or even used the aux tank. I think the first project I have to do is buy a new car. Have I ever said that before? It's quite warm and humid here, and I would like some A/C and a gas gauge. Can you imagine? A gas gauge. Such a luxury!*
>
> *This morning I plan to go to the office of housing to help me find an apartment. New students must live on campus for their first two years, but anyone over twenty-five or military personnel and veterans are exempt. Thank God for that. I couldn't live in a dorm with eighteen-year-olds. I'm used to being on my own.*
>
> *After I'm settled, registered, and have selected my classes, I plan to do some work on my search for Daffy*

Duck. Classes don't start until the Tuesday after Labor Day, so this gives me three weeks to organize. I also have to check in at the Naval Reserve Center.

Anyway, how are ya doin'? Send me a note. I miss you, but I'm sure we'll meet again; I'm sure.

Love you

The morning was bright, the sky clear, and the air still. The temperature promised to be in the upper eighties. A shower felt good, followed by clean clothes, with most items still packed in his suitcase and duffel bag. He grabbed his keys, locked the door to the room, and headed next door to have some breakfast at the IHOP. He didn't check out of the Comfort Inn because he would be there two or three more nights, but he was eager to find a permanent apartment.

He climbed in the bug and drove to the campus. The atmosphere there was clean and crisp, and the grounds were beautifully manicured. The campus had an educational feel, making a good impression. He had checked the campus map before leaving the motel. He immediately went to the department of housing.

"Good morning," the receptionist said with a smile. "How may I help you?"

"I'm a new student and a veteran. I'd like to inquire about living off campus, but I just happened to think, do I need an appointment?"

"No, you won't need an appointment. Right now, we're not busy. Do you have your enrollment credentials and military ID with you? Have you looked anywhere? Do you have anything in mind?"

Mike smiled. "That's three questions. Which one should I address first?"

The receptionist raised her head slightly and gave Mike a big smile. "Petty astute. How'd you learn that?"

"I used to train medical students at a university when I was in the Navy. It was teaching the art of communication. They quickly learned to ask only one question at a time."

"Sounds like you'll be good in English," replied the receptionist. "Let me get you over to one of our interviewers. Do you have your student ID card?"

"No, not yet."

"Okay, no problem. Go down the hall to the registrar's office. They will pull your application and take your photo, and you'll have your card in about ten minutes."

Mike went to the office, applied for a student ID, had his picture taken, and came back to the office of housing. He presented the information to the receptionist, and she said, smiling, "Please take a number and have a seat. You'll be next."

Actually, there was no one else waiting. The receptionist handed Mike some information about living off campus.

Mike took a seat and started to thumb through the information. About five minutes later, a woman came to the reception area. "Mr. Gibbons?"

"Yes," Mike replied, standing up with an outstretched hand.

"My name is Mariann, and I am here to help you with housing. Please come into my office. Do you have an interest in a particular dormitory?"

"I'd like to live off campus. I'm a veteran just released from active duty. I'm not sure I could live in a dormitory with eighteen-year-olds."

Mariann smiled, offering her hand and directing Mike to her desk. "Please have a seat. I'm not sure I could live with a group of eighteen-year-olds either."

"Please call me Mike."

"Thank you. And Mariann is spelled with an *i*. Do you have anywhere in mind where you would like to live?"

"No, I'm new to the area and have no idea where I'd want to be. I have to leave it up to you to help me."

"Please fill out this application and information sheet. There are four places I have in mind. You might be interested in going to each before making a decision."

Mariann gave Mike a list and description of the four possible apartment complexes approved by the university. He looked them over and said he would go this afternoon to look at each. He did not know where any of them were, but she assured him they were within proximity. She took out a map and marked the four locations.

"I see you have your student ID," she added. "Also, we'll need your DD 214 discharge paper and a copy of your birth certificate."

Mike had a strange feeling come over him once again. Just the mention of his birth certificate made him anxious. He felt uncomfortable about presenting it, but if the school wanted it, he would have to get it. If they asked any questions, he'd tell them the story. *What the hell?* he thought. *It's my life, and I didn't ask for it. It's just simply the way it is.*

"Sure. I can get both as soon as I unpack. They're packed with some other papers in a box. Do you need it before I move in somewhere?"

"No, so long as we have it within thirty days. That would be by the fifteenth of September."

"I'll see to it and get a man right on it. You will have it."

They both smiled. The first meeting seemed cordial and pleasant.

Mike went to the reception area, took a clipboard and pen, filled out the information sheet, and left it with the receptionist. He drove back to the Comfort Inn, changed into his shorts and T-shirt, and drove to a park nearby just a few blocks from the motel. He decided to search it out, as he had seen a couple of other runners using it when he'd passed it on the way to the university. He parked, put on his headphones, locked the car, and started out. It felt good to be out in the open, not thinking about going on duty. His thoughts turned to Mary and how he would like to have her here. *As soon as I finish my apartment searches this afternoon, I'll sit down and send her an e-mail.*

The run was great and gave Mike the energy he needed after the long drive. He drove back to the motel, where he put his damp shorts and T-shirt in a basin of soapy water. The shower felt great. It was always good to clean up and get on fresh clothes. He dressed in a pair of shorts and a polo shirt and decided to go for a quick lunch and get on with the apartment search. There was a Subway in the same mall as the IHOP. He sat down, ordered his usual tuna sandwich, and continued to look over the direction information for the four places.

16

The first one on the list was "Ravens View," an apartment complex not far from the university. He parked, went into the lobby, and saw a large woman sitting at a desk, smoking. The place smelled indescribably strong of cigarettes. *I don't know if she smokes Camels, but she looks like one—all old and wrinkled.* Mike turned around and left.

In about two miles, he came to "Pine Ridge Estates." What a name for a building in Florida. There were no pine trees, just palms, and no ridges either. The building was on a flat part of the landscape and appeared nicely manicured. He drove into the office parking spaces and thought, *If there is even a hint of cigarette smoke, I'm outta here.*

The lobby appeared clean, neat, and well kept. It had a scent of fresh pine. He went to the front desk. The information plaque stated the manager on duty was Ben Cartwright. There was no hint of cigarette smoke.

"Hi, can I help you?" Ben asked. He was pleasant and neat in his appearance.

"I'm starting at the university this fall, and I am looking for an apartment. You were recommended by the university's Department of Housing."

"Well, we do have students coming in, and we still have some available. There are a couple of options—a one-bedroom and also a one-bedroom with den. Are you looking for something furnished or unfurnished?"

"Furnished," Mike replied. "But may I see them both?"

"Absolutely."

Ben was a pleasant, fit-looking man of average height. He introduced his wife and asked her to guard the desk while he showed Mike the two available choices, both furnished.

Mike walked through the two apartments, exploring the kitchen and living room with the HD TV, couch, and other furnishings.

The rental fee for the one-bedroom was $400, but the management rented it to veterans for $350 a month, with one month's security deposit. The one-bedroom with den was $425 but $375 with the discount. For $20 extra, he could have clean sheets, towels, and a general cleaning once a week.

"*Sold!*" said Mike with a big smile. "When can I have it?"

"But which one do you want?"

Mike laughed and said, "The one with the den."

Ben smiled and could sense the excitement in Mike's body language. "Give us today to make sure everything is in working order. We'll re-clean it, and you can move on Friday afternoon."

"Oh, by the way, we do not allow smoking."

"That's fine by me. I have never smoked and never will."

"Okay. It's yours."

"Great! Help me out here. I have to buy a chest of drawers. Is there an unfinished furniture store around?" Ben directed Mike to the shopping mall a few blocks away.

"How about running? Anyplace nearby?"

"Yes, there's a running track down by the river. It's popular and peaceful, with a great coffee house nearby. There's also a cemetery just two blocks from here. They don't mind your running there, as long as you observe the dress code of wearing a shirt and also avoid funerals."

"Sounds great! Works for me."

Mike and Ben finished the paperwork and paid the deposit and first month's rent. He headed to the mall, bought a small chest with four drawers, and asked to have it delivered on Friday afternoon. Mike felt ahead of the game in getting ready for his college days.

He took his invoice with the measurements of the chest and went back to the Comfort Inn, planning to send Mary an e-mail.

As he booted the computer, he saw he had an e-mail from Mary:

Hey, Guy!

I've been thinking about you and how you are doing. Moving is such a pain.

You found an apartment yet? I know it takes time and worse when you are not familiar with the area. Lemme know how it all goes.

The work here is fine, but I miss my running partner. Stay in touch and good luck to you.

Miss you,

Mary

Mike returned the email right away.

Mary,

What a day I had. I finally found a great place to live. It's a large one-bedroom with a den, and it's furnished. It's $375 a month with a veteran's discount. I even have housekeeping service once a week for $20 extra. Can't beat that. The first place I went to, well, it was bad. I didn't bother to look at it. By bad, I mean it was full of stale cigarette smoke, and that's putting it mildly.

I think I'm gonna like it here. I move in on Friday, and I'm looking forward to getting settled. I wish you were here to help me with it. We could have a good time. It's different being alone and not knowing anyone, but I'm sure it will change once classes start.

Meanwhile, it's dinner time, and I'm heading to the beach tomorrow. I miss you. Maybe you could visit sometime.

Love you. Miss you too.

17

The wind must have changed direction, with the smell of bacon and sausage cooking from IHOP. Mike changed into his running gear, left his room at the Comfort Inn, and drove to the cemetery Ben had mentioned. A man working in a flower garden waved, and Mike noticed him. He figured the man was probably the caretaker, so he introduced himself and told him he would respect the cemetery rules. He put on his earphones and started out. During his run, he met another runner, a female. It reminded him of Mary and their meeting. They gave each other a smile, and a raised hand as they passed.

Back at the motel, Mike showered, changed clothes, and headed to the IHOP for a light breakfast. He took with him copies of the information sheets Joan Stevens had given him at the library. These extra two weeks would give him time to research and put together his plan for finding his father. He knew the first item he must take care of was his birth certificate. His determination was to fill in the spot where his father's name should be. He'd have to search in some boxes, as he didn't know which one contained the papers. His food arrived, so he put down his papers and downed three pancakes, two eggs, and sausage.

Delicious, he thought. *Light breakfast? Yeah, right!* It was close to eleven, and the beach called. The sun was now high in the sky, with few clouds.

He walked back to the motel and gathered his beach gear, chair, towel, and sunscreen. He'd get an umbrella at the beach stand. His thoughts turned to Mary, and he wished she could be there to put the lotion on his back. He didn't have plans for the day, except to register at the Naval Reserve facility.

He drove with the windows open. On his way, he saw a sign at a car lot. "Veterans and Military receive a 15 percent discount." He decided to drive in and take a look. He couldn't afford a new one. Actually, he could; he just didn't want to. The used car lot looked interesting; many cars were on display and available. As he toured the lot, a sales clerk named Bella came out and introduced herself. As they walked along making small talk about cars, he came upon a Honda Pilot. It was in great showroom condition. He and Bella took the Pilot for a spin, and he bought it. It was that easy.

Back in his VW, he headed for the causeway. He couldn't believe he had just bought a new car. It would be new to him, giving him the space he needed. Delivery would be the next day. The air felt good. He did have the luxury of a radio in the VW, so he had it on while he crossed the causeway. The air-conditioning was the open windows. The beach looked appealing, the sand like fine sugar. Mike thought he would take his shorts off, as he had his running gear on underneath and take a run down in the surf. He hadn't had his feet in the sand since earlier in the summer.

⁂

The trip to the Reserve unit was uneventful. The day was pleasant, and the traffic was somewhat heavy, but Mike relished the thought of getting a car with air-conditioning. He arrived at the Reserve office, checked in at the front desk, and waited for the processing. He had a two-year commitment remaining in the Reserves as part of his military contract. The reception room had a pleasant atmosphere, with flags of the United States neatly displayed, as well as award plaques in a glass-enclosed case. There was no hint of cigarette smoke. That pleased Mike.

A yeoman introduced himself as Jim Hansen, an enlisted member of the US Navy whose duties were clerical. Jim came out of the office and greeted Mike as he waited in the lobby. After a firm handshake and introductions, they settled down to the business of getting Mike transferred into in the unit. Mike presented Jim with his discharge paperwork.

"What brings you to Tampa?" Jim asked.

"I'm enrolled at the university and planning to study criminology. I'm interested in doing some genealogy research about my family. It takes time, but so far it's been fun."

Jim entered the information Mike had supplied. It was a quick and routine transaction. Right away, Mike felt welcome and was eager to join. He realized the next day would be a busy one. After he had met with his academic adviser at nine, he planned to go to the bank and pick up his cashier's check for the car. He'd call Bella to pick him up so he could drive her back. That way, he could pack the Pilot with his belongings. So much to do, so little time, but it was all coming together.

The yeoman finished the paperwork and put out his hand. "Welcome. It's good to have you here."

"Thanks. I think it'll work out just fine. I'm going to be a busy guy."

"Yes, you will. We meet every other Wednesday from seven to nine. Wear your whites until we change over to blues December first."

18

He went to his VW and drove several blocks from the reserve facility, with a hobby store in a strip mall coming up on the right. He pulled in, parked in the lot, grabbed the slip with the chest drawer measurements, and went inside. Mike had been entertaining an idea in his mind about the small metal box he'd carried with him since his high school days. It was always locked, with the key safely tucked away in his shaving kit. He wanted it to be more safe and sound and out of sight. He entered the store.

"Hello. Lemme know if I can be of help to you."

The clerk was a pleasant young man Mike figured to be in his early twenties.

"Yes, thanks. I need a piece of flat board like plywood but not heavy. Got anything like that?"

"We do. Follow me."

The clerk took Mike to an area of woodworking supplies, and they looked over several possibilities. He zeroed in on one.

"This is what I want, but I have no way of cutting it to the size I need."

"Not a problem," the young man replied. "We can cut you a piece to any size you want. You will only pay for what you want. Do you have the measurements?"

"Yes, right here." Mike handed the young man the invoice with the size he would need.

"We can do this. Is this the exact size of the drawer?"

"According to the invoice, yes. I want it to go inside the bottom of the bottom drawer I'll be using to hold some supplies I have for my classes at the university."

"I go to the university also. I'll be a sophomore studying general business administration. How about you? Are you just starting?"

"Yes, I'm a first year. I just got off active duty in the Navy. I plan to study criminology."

"A police officer?" the clerk asked.

"Nope. Just someone who does investigative work."

"Great. Maybe we'll meet on campus sometime. My name's Andy."

"And I'm Mike."

They shook hands and continued.

"Now. About your piece of wood. I would recommend about a sixteenth of an inch less on each side so it would fit. Otherwise, if you cut it exactly the size of the box, it may not go in so smoothly. The drawer may not be perfectly square." Andy hesitated, looked at Mike with a slight smile, and said, "What you think?"

"Me thinks you have a good point. I take it you're not an English major."

Chuckling, "Are you kidding? I didn't do well in English. I can only read, write, and speak the English language." They both laughed, and Andy continued. "I'll plan to cut you a piece to these measurements less an eighth on each side. So, if you bring the drawer in, I can make a custom fit. I'll be working all day tomorrow if you want to do it then. I think it would be the easiest."

"Sounds great. Let's give it a shot."

Mike left the hobby store. Because it was mid-afternoon, he decided to stop at the bank and pick up his cashier's check for the car. The bank wasn't busy, so he saw one of the personal bankers right away.

The inheritance from his grandma and his savings from the Navy came in handy, with change left over. The check was ready, and he left.

Mike had work to do when he arrived back at the apartment. He was confident the shelf would fit, but he wanted to make sure. He decided that, once the Pilot arrived, he would take the bottom drawer back to the hobby store and have it cut so it would fit. Andy was a great help and knew exactly what Mike wanted. Now he had to devise a way to lock the drawer. He went online and started searching. He found a small locking device that would allow the entire mechanism to be on the underside of the fitted piece of wood. The lock would require four digits of the owner's choosing to unlock it. He placed the order. The device would arrive in two days.

19

Mike found Dr. Greene's office easily. He knocked on the partially open door at eight fifty-nine.

"Come in," a gruff voice called out from inside the room.

A musty odor greeted Mike as he opened the door. One side of the room had floor-to-ceiling shelves stacked with old books. It looked like a used bookstore filled with nothing but old antique treasures which Dr. Greene probably hadn't taken off the shelf for who knows how long. The light was bright through the curtainless window. You could see dust particles floating in the rays of the sun. The only lighting in the darker hours would be a ceiling light with a fan attached. The fan was off; the room, stuffy and warm. Dr. Greene, a bearded man in his mid to late-sixties wore glasses of a '50s era and his hair disheveled and long below the collar of his wrinkled shirt. He looked like he'd slept in his clothes the night before. *Ah! The Einstein of the educational world.* The desk, loaded with papers, made Mike wonder if Dr. Greene knew where everything was. He'd bet he did. Dr. Greene greeted Mike with an arm outstretched. They shook hands, and he offered Mike a seat.

"Good morning, sir," Mike started, introducing himself.

Dr. Greene remained seated and didn't introduce himself or state his name.

The professor looked over his half glasses, which were full of dandruff and fingerprints. He picked up Mike's file and opened it to the first page. "Mike Gibbons, fresh out of the Navy, ready to take on studies here at the university." Dr. Greene spoke slowly and with a mild-mannered voice. "First, I want to say, I am impressed with your punctuality."

"Thank you, sir. Just having spent four years in the military makes me aware of being punctual. I pride myself on it."

Dr. Greene nodded approvingly. "Well, I have all of your paperwork and your high school transcript. You should do well in your studies here. We have many military students enrolled who develop a maturity while in the service. Let's talk about your program and the courses you will have to take to get your degree." Dr. Greene went on to introduce Mike to the general requirements and then the specific studies in criminology.

"I also see you were a top-notch wrestler in high school. Did you do any follow-up while in the Navy?"

"No, sir. There was no program in which I could take part. I would have if there had been, as I like the sport."

"Now please, I recognize your courtesy, but you do not have to address me as 'sir.' I am just plain ole Bob Greene. You are not a teenager, and I give you permission to address me as Bob."

"I guess it's just the habit of the Navy, but well-taken. Addressing you as Bob will take some time."

"I want you to know, I don't give all my students the same permission. Only to military."

"Thank you, si …" Mike smiled, shaking his head.

Dr. Greene kept a straight face, looking over his dandruff and fingerprinted glasses. As he turned to set the papers down, the sun shined on his glasses.

How does he see anything through those?

"Now back to the intramural wrestling. It might interest you to know we have several programs here. There are young men and women coming out of high school and the military who were in baseball, football, track and field, swimming, various athletic teams, and I could

The Day Always Comes

go on and on. They all would like to keep up the sport, but may not qualify or don't want to qualify for the varsity teams. Wrestling is also one of them. If students want to continue with the sport, we allow them to form intramural teams. It's popular, and if you're interested, I'll give you the name of the director of the program."

"I'd like that. It would also allow me to meet other guys who share the same interest in the sport. I might be a little rusty, but I've kept up my physical strength since high school. I feel I'm in good shape."

"It would also give you the opportunity to work with high school students, as the coaches are always looking for assistants. They would pay you as well."

"I would like that also. I'd enjoy working with teenagers. Wrestling is a sport that develops character, maturity, and discipline."

"Okay, I'll do it, and let's complete your curriculum in criminology. I want to give you an outline of the four years. It can, and probably will, change as time passes. You'll start with the basics—English, math, general science …"

Dr. Greene went on to set up a program for Mike over the next four years and register him in his freshman courses. It sounded like a heavy and intense load, which would have him drowning in work, but Mike realized he would approach it little by little.

"I plan to go to summer school if that makes a difference."

"Excellent. You'll get through quicker, and besides, summer school tuition is lower. I think this should give you an idea of where we need to go, and I'll contact Tom Baylee about the intramural wrestling. I think you'll like him and will enjoy it. He's always looking for new blood." Dr. Greene hesitated. "Well, maybe that's not a good word to use in wrestling. Just looking at you, I realize I would not want to mess with you." They both smiled and chuckled. "Good luck to you during your time here at the university. I think you'll like it."

"Thank you, … Bob. Good meeting you, and if I have any difficulty, I'll be in contact."

Mike and Dr. Greene stood, the two shook hands, and Mike left.

That was tough addressing him as Bob. He's a character, but I liked him. I don't know how he can stand to work in that disorganized office, though.

20

It was almost ten o'clock. Mike had some time to himself. As he walked out of the faculty office building, he saw the library directly across the street and decided to go in. He wanted to continue his research into his father, and he needed to put together a plan of action. So far, he only had information, not a plan. The front desk clerk greeted him, and Mike asked to see the librarian. The clerk directed him to Arlene McDaniel, opposite the reception desk.

Mike approached Arlene. She had a delightful smile, short-cropped hair, and wore very little, if any, makeup. She raised her head with a smile. "Good morning. How can I help you?"

Mike smiled. "I would say I'm looking for my father, but that would be misleading. You see, I had a wonderful mother who brought me into this world with the help of a donor. I'd like to find him. If I do, I plan to present a paper about my search."

"Wonderful," she replied. "This is not a new question. There are others all over this world who are seeking the same. Do you have your library card handy?"

"I don't have one yet. I'm a new student just starting my undergraduate year. I have my student ID, but that's all so far. I met with my adviser this morning, and he enrolled me in my classes."

"Well, let's go over to the front desk and get you signed up. The card will give you access to your search."

They walked over. Mike filled out the application and had his picture taken. The card was printed out in about thirty seconds.

"Now let's go over to the section where we keep the information you'll be seeking."

"Thanks so much. I'll just browse through this area and become familiar with what's here. Also, I would like to start using the Internet."

"You can, and there is information directing you to helpful websites. I also can assist you with it. If you have any questions, I am here. Please don't hesitate to ask. The only dumb question is the one that is never asked."

Mike looked at the librarian, they both smiled, and she returned to her desk.

Picking through the books in the section she'd directed him to, he came across one titled *The Central Register*. It contained several chapters on reproductive technology, instructions for donors, and information on surrogacy, as well as voluntary information and instructions to begin your search.

As he browsed, he sensed a man a few feet away and behind him. As Mike moved about, he could tell the man was looking at him, but he didn't respond to his presence. Mike continued his search through the large volume of information on one shelf, and it delighted him to have an outline of the work ahead. There were several websites in which he became interested.

Mike approached the checkout desk, and as he did, the man near him walked out as well. He turned and looked at Mike. Mike looked at him. He was tall, about Mike's height, nicely dressed, and wearing a baseball cap with a Detroit Tigers logo and a pair of Ray-Ban sunglasses. Mike made eye contact with him long enough to register and sink into the moment, turned back, and wondered, *Is this guy trying to pick me up? If he is, he's headed in the wrong direction*. He checked out the materials and left the library, not seeing the man he thought was following him, and headed back to the motel.

The Day Always Comes

※

He had packed his bags the night before so he could check out and move to the apartment the next morning. Bella was coming with the Pilot at eleven thirty. He would take her to lunch and then back to work. He took the VW to the apartment; Bella would pick him up there.

Bella and the car arrived; it was beautiful. It looked brand new and not pre-owned, as they car dealers call them. Mike and Bella had a fun lunch at the Olive Garden. He took her back to the office, gave her the check and drove off.

Back at the motel, Mike packed the pilot, checked out, and drove to the apartment. With everything moved from the motel to his apartment, he settled in, unpacked, and was ready for the chest of drawers.

After the chest was delivered in the early afternoon, he put the bottom drawer in the Pilot and drove to the hobby shop to have Andy size it for a proper fit. It was perfect.

Over the next few days, he worked on getting organized and bought the books and supplies he would need. Of course, he continued to run every day.

He received a call from Tom Baylee about the intramural wrestling program. Tom said he was delighted to get a new guy on the team and so glad you would be working with high school wrestlers. He would be in touch.

Mike also spent time filling in forms of inquiry to send in his search for his father. He sent them off to the county clerk in Washtenaw County, his birthplace in Michigan.

A week later, Mike sold the VW for a thousand dollars

21

During Mike's freshman year, he spent time with the intramural wrestling team and students from Central High who wanted to remain in shape for the season. Classes started, and he was a busy man. Everything had gone very well. After two weeks, he looked in the mirror while shaving and said, "What the hell have I gotten myself into?" There were English essays and basic computer skills, on an Apple no less. Mike was a PC guy. Life had now been all about new learning. He had economics to read and research to do, an algebra quiz to get ready for, and work to do in Sociology 101, the beginning course of three years of work. Then on Wednesday evening's every other week, he had to take time for the Reserve meetings. He wondered early in the ball game if he had taken on too much.

For his sociology course, he was required to spend time with the homeless. There were several choices, and he selected St. Ben's because it was a short distance from his apartment. He drove there and had been told by his sociology professor the director and personnel at the shelter were expecting him, so he wasn't nervous.

Opening the big door, he soon spotted a man behind the counter in the corner. "Hi, I'm Mike Gibbons."

"Oh yeah, Mike, nice to meet you. I'm Matt Ryan. Your sociology professor spoke highly of you. I'll be assisting you, and I think this should work out well."

The Day Always Comes

They shook hands. Mike looked around the large room containing used furniture, tables, chairs, computers, telephones, and a snack area with coffee and rolls.

"In about five minutes, I'll open the door, so prepare yourself," Matt said with a big smile. Mike had no idea what would happen.

༒

Matt opened the front door promptly at nine o'clock. About sixty to seventy-five people entered with an ear-pounding clobber of sound, moving forward like a crowd at a department store sale the day after Christmas. Many of the guests wore lightweight clothes, looking like they'd slept in them all night. Matt assured him they probably had.

Mike watched as the homeless and hungry, young and old, men and women, crowded around the desk asking for vaseline to use on their dry and chapped hands and lips. They wanted chessboards, checkerboards, domino pieces, playing cards, and numbers for the selective take-a-number-and-have-a-seat use of the telephone. The chitchat noise of, "I want," "I need," and, "where is," dominated the area. People were talking, and staff calling out names. The smell of coffee wafted over the line of unshaven men and women with uncombed hair asking if they had any mail. For most, St. Ben's was their only mailing address, and they were happy to be there—their home for the day.

A man looked directly at Mike. His beard was stubble of several days; his face, neck, and hands were dirty. He was in need of a shower. His teeth were black and out of alignment. "I need some clean socks. My feet are cold and wet." There had been thunderstorms during the night.

Matt replied in a kind but firm voice while waving the index finger of his hand back and forth. "You have to wait until nine fifteen. No socks before that time. You know the rules, Jim."

"Yeah, I know, but it's worth a try." His bare feet touched the floor; they appeared wet, red, and sore.

"He thought he'd get a pair because you're new," Matt said to Mike with a smile on his face. "Ya gotta watch 'em; they may be homeless, but they aren't dumb, and they'll pull any string they can, especially if they realize you're new."

Mike smiled and nodded his head, "Yeah, it's also because I don't know the rules."

Just then, a nicely dressed man approached Matt and Mike.

"Good morning, Matt," he said.

"Hey, good morning Dr. Ben," Matt replied.

"Mike, I'd like you to meet our in-house doctor, Dr. Ben Kelly, better known as, Dr. Ben."

The doctor came in twice a week to care for those with coughs, colds, sores, and any number of medical issues interfering with the residents' daily lives. He'd adopted the name Ben because of the name of the home—St. Ben's.

"Hi. I'm Mike Gibbons, the new kid around here."

"Pleasure to meet you. What brings you to St. Ben's?"

The doctor was tall and neatly dressed, and Mike guessed him to be in his late fifties or early sixties.

Mike had a feeling he had seen Dr. Ben before. He looked so familiar, but Mike could not place the event or when it had occurred, if it ever had. His mind searched for the connection, but he finally shook the feeling of familiarity off as coincidence. The two shook hands in a greeting that was rather awkward. Mike realized they were both left-handed and that he was staring at the doctor. Dr. Ben stared at Mike also. It was a strange meeting.

Mike replied, "I'm a sophomore at the university. I have to do a semester of outside work for my sociology class at a place for the homeless and create an essay, which will be due before my senior year finishes. St. Ben's was one of the places on the list; it's convenient for me."

"Well, if there's anything I can do to help, let me know. What days do you plan to be here?"

"I think Tuesdays and Fridays from nine until noon."

"Same as me."

They had only just met, but still, there was a familiar look about Dr. Ben that Mike could not place.

"Have we met before?" Mike asked. "You look so familiar to me."

They both smiled. Dr. Ben just shook his head and dropped the subject. "People have said that to me before," Dr. Ben replied. Mike thought maybe his asking was a bit too presumptuous.

"Let me tell you how I decided to come here," Dr. Ben continued. "I had a clinic for many years. For health reasons, my wife and I moved, and I joined a group not far from here. I drove past St. Ben's on my way to and from the clinic every day. There would always be a line of people every morning winding around the building, rain or shine. I never gave it much thought; these were just homeless people, waiting to get in. Sometimes I would recall for a moment how I woke up every morning in my warm bed. I shave; shower; and put on clean clothes, clean socks, and a good fitting pair of shoes. I make my coffee with freshly ground beans, read the paper in comfort, and eat a bowl of cereal with fresh fruit. I didn't feel guilty, just compassion. How about you?"

"This will be an eye-opener for me. I'm just starting out in life. I got out of the Navy a little over a year ago and started my education in criminology."

"Great! I admire you for doing your service. What did you do in the Navy?"

"I was a member of the shore patrol and worked at the main gate of the naval hospital. My main course of study was that of hospital corpsman."

Dr. Ben pursed his lips, smiled, and raised his hand, pointing his index finger at Mike. "I may need an assistant, as the number of patients is getting larger. Would you be interested in helping out?"

"Definitely! I'd love to."

"We'll plan on seeing each other each week. Let's get a bite to eat next Tuesday after work, and we can talk about working together."

That was right up Mike's alley—he did enjoy eating out. "Sounds good to me. I'll plan on it. Do you have a current practice?"

"I've retired as a physician. I've had a wonderful profession in dermatology, doing what I wanted to do in life, but thirty-five years in the practice was enough. Besides, I was diagnosed with a heart murmur several years ago, and now it has developed into atrial fibrillation."

"That's interesting. I also have a heart murmur, diagnosed when I had my exit physical from the Navy. I don't think I have atrial fibrillation, however."

Raising his hands, palms up like he was begging for money, Dr. Ben continued, "Well, we have something in common to talk about already. I'm here at St. Ben's because I loved my occupation, but now I figure it's time to give something back. I work here as a volunteer physician a couple of days a week, give health care to those who can't afford it. But their world is a new world to me, something I've never experienced."

Dr. Ben and Mike smiled at each other.

"Now if you'll excuse me, I have an office, if you want to call it that, and I already have some patients waiting. We'll talk again."

"Sure. I'll plan for next Tuesday."

Mike turned around and thought to himself, *Hmm, a heart murmur. It'll be interesting to compare notes.* It suddenly struck him; *Dr. Ben is my height, we are both left-handed, we part our hair on the right side, and we both have blue eyes. Then the heart murmurs? Something is fitting into this puzzle of my life. I wonder. Yes, I wonder.*

22

One day before classes started, Mike picked up his mail. There was an envelope from the county clerk's office in Michigan. He quickly opened it and read the enclosed letter:

> *Dear Mr. Gibbons,*
>
> *We received your letter and application for information about finding your donor father. Enclosed you will find a document about your request. You will notice the name of your father shows "unknown." This entry is normal and accepted as legal when the father, as you have marked on your application, is a donor.*
>
> *We also have your application for locating your father. It has taken some time, but searching the normal channels, we have determined he is still alive. We could obtain his record, the date and place of donation, and where he is now. However, he left specific instructions. His identity is to remain sealed until six months after his death. The donor has the right to remain unknown for a period he chooses, even until after the donor's death or never.*
>
> *Your donor listed many reasons for his request not to be known, and we must respect his directive. After some*

research, we have filed a request for his identity, as per his directive, and death certificate when it becomes available.

The information and your application will remain on file, and when we discover his death through legal channels, we will notify you. Please keep your current address updated with us, as we will send the requested information to your last address on file.

Very truly yours,
James J. Herald
Office of the County Clerk,
Washtenaw County
Ann Arbor, Michigan

Mike stood and spoke quietly out loud. "It's one damn thing after another. You can't do this. You can't do that. You have to wait." He recalled what Joan had said about his search. "It could be difficult; it could be easy," He was finding this difficult. *But, he reminded himself, progress is being made.*

He looked back down at the letter and shook his head, correcting himself. Progress *had been* made. Now he seemed to have come to a dead end. An expression of disappointment crossed his face. He'd hoped his inquiry would receive better news. He remembered more of Joan Stevens's words: "Assume nothing. Expect nothing. You may find nothing. Your search could be long and complicated."

Mike immediately sat down and wrote and mailed his current address to James Herald, the county clerk in Ann Arbor, Michigan.

He decided to go for a run. This time, instead of going to the cemetery, he would go down by the river, where the scenery was better. Somehow the cemetery seemed a bit morbid.

Just the drive to the river made him feel more alert, and as he drove, he told himself, *Forget it for now. Forget about the past. The day will come when I will have the whole puzzle put together. Maybe I'll be sorry when*

The Day Always Comes

I learn my father's background, maybe not. And right now, it's suspenseful and exciting. But I have the key in my shaving kit, and I wish I could get rid of it. The day will come. Mike smiled and said out loud, "The day always comes."

He parked his Honda Pilot, put in the earplugs to his iPhone, stretched, and started the run. The air was fresh; it felt good. The only activity on the river was that of rowing crews practicing—two teams of eight in separate sculls. Their pace made patterns in the calm water, like contrails circling from the wings of jet airplanes.

It would be three miles to the next bridge, where he would cross the river and return from the other side. It was just a short run for him, only six miles. He liked being alone. No questions, no one in his space. It was his time, and he could think. After all, there would be no one to argue with him or try to change his mind. Also, when he was alone, he realized how his mind was not clear. He thought about his past life. He was happy with what he had accomplished and looked forward to his future, but there was a past transgression that weighed heavily on his shoulders. The key. He loved his grandma and how she had raised him. He still cherished the picture of him as a three-year-old sitting on his mother's lap.

He often wondered what his father looked like. He'd thought about it many times. *Did he have hair like mine?* He would find himself wondering, even though he knew from his Biology/Genetics 101 courses that a man's hair genetically resembled that of his mother's father. The picture of his grandfather showed a likeness.

◎◎

A month had gone by since Mike had received the letter from the county clerk in Michigan. He faithfully worked two days a week from nine till noon at St. Ben's. He'd come to know more people who occupied the same seats every day and started giving them medical attention once he'd started working with Dr. Ben. Some residents may not have received an immunization in years. They arrived with coughs, fever, upper respiratory infections, cardiac conditions, and nutrition problems.

Some, he could tell, had distinct marks on their arms. They obviously were active drug users. Mike talked with them. They were happy to tell him they were clean. Blood tests might tell a different story.

23

His junior year completed, Mike only had one more to go and was doing well with his studies. He enjoyed college and the university. Summer was in full bloom, and Mike started his running routine as the days became warmer. He reminded himself, *Only one year left starting this fall, and I'm on my own.*

He changed his running pattern to the river walk, even though it was farther away than the nearby cemetery. He met many other runners, dog walkers, and bikers on the path, and running there became a more mind refreshing experience. Besides, on the way from the spot where he did his sprints, he discovered a pastry shop. It became a habit for him to stop for a cup of coffee on the way back to his apartment. Other runners and bikers frequented the shop, and over the past three years, he started meeting people with his same interests. The smell of fresh coffee and the freshly baked pastries was always inviting. Sitting outside as the days became warmer was fun, allowing him to get away from his studies. He also met other classmates who were also taking courses in the summer. He would complete his course requirements and graduate in June of the next year.

Mike also enjoyed going to the Coffee and Pastry Hut, known as the C & P because the woman behind the counter was always so pleasant and soon said she looked forward to Mike's coming in. One especially bright, sunny day, he stopped with a couple of his friends. As his friends were ordering from one of the other servers, Mike smiled at the woman behind the counter.

"Good morning," he said. "For as long as we've spoken to each other, I think it's time we knew each other's names. I'm Mike Gibbons."

"Well, I think it's about time also." She spoke with a crisp, British accent. "I'm Sylvia. Sylvia Dunn," she replied, extending her hand and tipping her head to one side in a gesture of pleasantness. She had a sweet face; a nice smile; and beautiful gray hair that looked like she had just come from the hairdresser.

"I have noticed you have a British accent. Are you from England?"

"I am indeed. Cornwall, in the southwest near Land's End. Are you familiar with England?"

"I am, only to the extent where I can recognize it on the map. Someday I wish to go there. But I need to get my education behind me."

"Well, I think you would enjoy it, indeed. Lovely it is. Now, what would you like this morning?"

"All of your pastries are so delicious and smell so good."

"I brought all the recipes with me when I came here seven years ago. Have you tried my saffron bread?"

"Not yet, but I will. But meanwhile, I believe I will celebrate England and have a cup of coffee and a scone," he said, pointing to the tray in the case.

"Now a true Brit would have a cup of tea with their scone, smothered with clotted cream."

Mike sucked in his breath between his teeth and said, "I never drink tea except in the summer, and it's only ice tea. And clotted cream? That's a heart-stopper."

"Well I nevah," she said with a smile. "I shall have to work on fixing that. Now let me fetch your order. I have some fresh scones in the kitchen. I shall get you one straight away." Sylvia turned and went into the kitchen. She returned with a warm, fresh scone on a plate. "Here is your coffee and a fresh scone, and today it's on me."

"Well thank you, Sylvia. I'll see you again, and somehow, I shall repay you. I'll be back."

"You coming in often will be payment enough. But I must ask you, do you know why we call the far western tip of England, Land's End?"

Mike stood perplexed. "I've heard of Land's End, but I have no idea why it's called that."

"Because anything further would be Scilly." Sylvia laughed.

Mike just stood there. He wore an expression of puzzlement, but a smile as well. He thought, *Am I missing something?*

"Mike, you must get out a map of England and look to the west of Land's End. Now, you go outside and enjoy the day."

"Thank you again, and I'll see you tomorrow."

Mike left the coffee shop, went outside, and sat at a table with some friends. The sun was warm, and the coffee and the scone, perfect.

24

Mike continued to work at St. Ben's. During the summer months he volunteered and became good friends with Dr. Ben. The two of them had a good routine worked out at the clinic, and the doctor relied on Mike for his expertise and experience and because he quickly picked up new skills.

On the Wednesday evenings when he had Reserve duty, he would eat early and make sure his uniform was clean and pressed. The drive to the Reserve station put him in a not so great or desirable part of town. He had become aware of that right from the start and would always make sure he locked the Pilot and placed his cell phone out of sight.

One meeting during the summer months, he arrived early and locked up. Many of the Reserves had already arrived, and after mustering, he went to the clinic where he and Dr. Marty McGraw, the dentist, worked together. They told stories and engaged in conversation until it was time to leave.

After the meeting, Mike went to his car. A man popped out in front of the hood, and it surprised Mike. The man was young, probably in his early twenties, and had a knife. He extended his hand with the knife and pointed it at Mike's face. "Give me the keys, swabbie, and don't pull any tricks. I'm good with this, and you ain't gonna be lookin' pretty when I'm done with you."

Mike dropped the keys close to the young man and in front of him. He put his hands up level with his chest as if to indicate, *Stop*.

"Why are you doing this? You're young and have a good life ahead of you. You can have my car. It's yours. Just leave me alone."

"Pick up the keys, sailor." The young man was rough, agitated, and meant what he said.

Mike hesitated and slowly bent over with the palms of his outstretched hands facing down. This was a trick he'd learned from his wrestling days; it allowed him to grab his opponent with open hands. Just then, the attacker stepped back, and Mike knew this was the time to attack. He grabbed the young man's right leg with his dominant left hand and raised it waist high, causing his attacker to lose his balance. Within seconds, Mike slid the heel of his right foot behind the left ankle of the perpetrator. It was all done quickly and with expert precision. The knife flew out of the young man's hand as he lost his balance and tried to stop his fall. Mike thought about his wrestling days and his last match with Jim Louis.

"You are really stupid, do you know that? You should be careful and selective who you mess with. I'm an expert wrestler. I'm not going to hurt you, but I will get some 9-1-1 help just for you, and let the police handle this."

He grabbed the young man by the belt on the backside of his pants, making things a little tight, and then by the neck of his shirt in the back, like a horse collar tackle in football. The would-be thief tried to use his hands to free himself, but Mike had him far enough off the ground so his hands wouldn't be useful in an attempt to escape. The young man was yelling and kicking. Mike knew exactly how to handle it. He jerked strongly on his belt, tightening his trousers and shorts. "Shut up, or your voice will permanently change," Mike added.

"Hey, what's going on, Mike?" one of his fellow Navy guys asked as a group of them stepped out of the building.

"This guy wanted to steal my car. There's a knife on the ground next to the Pilot at the left front wheel, along with my car keys. Call the police for me, would you?"

One of the men in his unit ran inside the building. Mike put the young man on the ground facedown.

"You move, and you're dead meat, and I mean it," Mike said in a firm voice. "Dead meat doesn't mean I will kill you. It means you won't like what you look like the rest of your life."

Just then, some of the other Reserves came out of the building. "The cops are on their way," one said.

The police arrived within five minutes. They knew this young man. He had a record. The police officers put handcuffs on him and escorted him to the back seat of the patrol car. Mike explained what had happened, and the officers went over to the Pilot. One picked up the knife by the tip of the blade, putting it in a plastic evidence bag.

"I'll have to ask you to come to the station to fill out a report."

"Not a problem," Mike said. "I'll follow you."

Mike picked up his keys and followed the squad car to the precinct station.

25

The next day was the beginning of fall classes. The summer was fleeing by, and Mike went to work at St. Ben's twice a week as planned. He had a paper to do to wrap up his sociology studies, and he thought Dr. Ben would be the perfect person to ask for help with this project. He had come to know the doctor over the past two years, and he had spoken about his wife only once. Her name was Maria, and Mike had never met her or even seen her. Dr. Ben said she was Italian, and he'd met her in Pittsburg years ago. Her husband had died, accidentally, and they'd become friends. That's all Mike knew about her.

Mike got up early, shaved, showered, and dressed. A message on his phone asked him to stop into the police station at his convenience to sign the final paperwork about the night before. The officer pointed out this was not the young man's first incident with the law. Mike decided to go to the station after he finished his day's work at St. Ben's.

With his senior year beginning today, it was going to be a busy morning. Dr. Ben was already setting up for the morning rush. They greeted each other, and Mike put out the usual items needed to treat the guests. He decided it was time to ask if the doctor would work with him on a project for sociology.

The two of them were the only ones there so Mike thought it a perfect time to have a discussion. "Dr. Ben, I have to interview a professional person and write an essay on the interview. This paper will be my final work for my sociology class. We've known each other for two years, and I feel comfortable with you and respect you. Would you be willing to agree to an anonymous interview? I will not mention your name." Mike said. Smiling, he held up a hand and added, "Please feel free to say no."

Dr. Ben put the thumb of his left hand under his chin, his index finger over his lips and placed his eyes in a down position. Then he looked back up at Mike. "So, you've always addressed me formally as Dr. Ben. I would be glad to, only if I can read it before you turn it in. And thank you for agreeing not to mention my name. We have worked together for two years. I have never revealed my real name to you or anyone else, for that matter. So from now on, my name is not Dr. Ben. Address me as Aaron."

Mike straightened up, tipped his head, smiled, and opened his mouth slightly. "I have always known you as Dr. Ben. I have always seen you sign the medical reports as Dr. Ben Kelly. My not knowing your true name is no big deal to me. You can be anyone you want to be," he said with a smile and a chuckle in his voice. "You do not look like an Aaron to me. You will always look like a Dr. Ben, so I say to you, agreed." They shook hands.

Aaron seemed relaxed and happy. Mike accepted the news as an epiphany of sorts. "Where and when can we meet in private to begin?" he asked. "I don't know if I can complete this in a single session. Would you be willing to meet more than once?"

"Sure," Aaron replied. "We could meet at Starbucks on Division Street for starters. After that, it would probably be just short times. I am happy to help you."

"Thank you so much," Mike said. "I didn't know who else to ask at this point."

"You're welcome."

"Are you free anytime tomorrow? I'm off until noon. I have a class starting at one o'clock."

"Tomorrow around nine thirty would be ideal for me. How about you?"

"I'll see you at nine thirty tomorrow at Starbucks on Division."

Mike went on with his work for the day, helping men shower and get clean clothes, especially socks. The barber would be coming in tomorrow, and Mike wouldn't be there, but there was a list of men wanting haircuts. The two volunteer barbers had a good time together and had gotten to know St. Ben's well. Mike thought, *It feels good to see the poor cleaned up with fresh everything.*

26

Mike left to meet Aaron at nine thirty the next morning. He took his laptop, a pad of paper, and some pens with him. He found a table in a corner by the window where the light would not reflect on his computer screen and where the two of them could speak in private. Aaron showed up a few minutes later. They ordered coffee and a roll, sat down, and started.

Aaron was the first to speak. "I don't know where you want to begin, so why don't I just tell you where I was growing up and where I am today, with a few bumps in the road along the way."

"You start wherever you'd like. You can ramble on. I can piece together your thoughts to make a chronology," Mike replied.

"I guess I should start with where I am now. As I told you yesterday, my name isn't Ben. It's Aaron Kelly. I'm a retired dermatologist from Pittsburg. I chose the name Dr. Ben because of the day home for the homeless. Working at St. Ben's, Dr. Ben just seemed to fit."

It didn't matter to Mike if the man he'd come to admire said his name was Joe, Pete, Tom, or Aaron. He would always be Dr. Ben to Mike. He smiled and thought the nickname clever. "Where did you grow up?" he asked, poised to type out Dr. Ben's answer.

"Born and raised in Pittsburgh, graduated from Princeton, and went to Washington University in St. Louis. I followed up with some studies at the University of Michigan. After graduation, I did my residency at Yale and started my dermatology practice back in Pittsburgh. We were a poor family. Or maybe I should say, we got along just fine, but never had any extra income. I have a brother who was always the big man on campus. He was the shining star of the family. I was the guy who lived in my head."

"What do you mean 'lived in your head'?"

"Well, it was always Dungeons and Dragons, mythology and stuff, knights in shining armor saving damsels in distress." Aaron talked on and on, telling Mike how his brother was the fair-haired boy in the family.

Aaron also told him about how he always liked reading books about flying and fantasizing. "My SAT and ACT scores were excellent, so I graduated from high school with a scholarship."

Mike nodded his head, looked at Aaron, and said, "I suppose without that scholarship, you would not have been able to afford college. You said your family was poor. What did you do for income? Did you work?"

"I wouldn't have been able to go to college without some extra spending money." Aaron stopped and stared straight ahead. He opened his mouth, but nothing came out. "I have never told anyone this," he finally said, "but …" Aaron hesitated.

There was silence. Mike looked up, and Aaron was looking out the window as if in deep thought.

"I don't know if I should tell you this. I guess I shouldn't go there." Aaron shook his head, pursed his lips and said, "Oh, never mind."

"Well, it's out of the bag now," Mike said. "Remember, I will not reveal your name or anything about this conversation—ever." Mike put his pencil down and closed his computer.

Aaron looked back at Mike and stared for a bit. He opened his mouth and took a deep breath. "For me to have some extra cash when I was at Michigan, I would go to the bulletin boards in the student union and other places on campus to see what I could do to earn extra money. Various departments at the university and sometimes private organizations were always looking for students to take part in various studies, and they often paid for it."

"That's true. I've seen those notices. I've often thought of doing some of them myself." Mike hesitated. "What did you do?"

"As I said, I have never told anyone about this—no one." Aaron hesitated again, took in a deep breath, looked Mike in the eyes, and said, "I made sperm donations at $150 a pop. It was a good way for me to earn the extra money. It was a no-brainer. I never told my parents or anyone about it. You are the first to know."

Mike sat and looked at Aaron, almost paralyzed. A chill came over his body. Both of them were left-handed had blond hair and blue eyes; they were the same height; and then there was the heart murmur. *Is he?* Mike couldn't help but ask himself. *He went to the University of Michigan. I grew up close to Ann Arbor. I don't know, but somehow I'm going to find out. I'm beginning to think he is.* Mike's head started spinning. He wasn't listening, but he came back to the present moment shortly as Aaron continued talking.

As Aaron talked, giving his history, Mike only looked straight ahead here and there, occasionally looking at Aaron. Aaron's statement was a spellbinding admission. Mike drew into himself. He could hear talking in the background, but he wasn't paying attention.

Aaron continued, "The point you have to understand about my family is that my father played football in college, but he was a small man then, and he never made the pros." Aaron hesitated, sensing Mike was somewhere else in his thoughts. "Are you with me? Hell-lo! Mike, you seem a little distant right now. Are you getting fatigued?" Aaron waved his hand in front of Mike's face.

"No, no, not ... I was ... I ... I'm just thinking about how to put this all together." He waved his left hand in between the two of them and shook his head from side to side. "It's ... it's; this is intriguing," Mike said. "It sounds as though you were always playing second fiddle to your brother." Mike was beside himself. His mind was racing.

"Well, yes, and there's more. Hey, do you see what time it is? You wanted to be out of here by noon. It's a quarter till. Maybe we can continue this at another time. I have to say, Mike, I enjoyed laying out my life to you. It's something I have never done. I have never been able to do it. No one knows but you. It feels good to be able to talk about it."

Mike thanked Aaron for his time, and they decided to meet the next week. Mike had said he had a class, but actually, he didn't, and he was glad he didn't. He'd just wanted to be sure the interview didn't go on and on and on.

27

Mike went to his Pilot. The drive from Starbucks was slow, as he had quite a bit on his mind. After arriving at his apartment, Mike put his computer and materials on the desk and stared out the window. *I wonder*, he thought. He changed and went back down to his car to go over by the river. He sat on a hill facing the water. Somehow, he needed to filter all the thoughts going through his mind. *Could he be? I don't know. I need to figure it out, but I have to do it in a methodical manner.*

Just take it step by step, he cautioned himself. *I can't rush and make it a monkey on my back.*

Go slow, Mike, he thought.

Is he my biological father? He chuckled to himself. "Daffy Duck," he said softly.

Go slow, he cautioned again. *We are so similar. But I've waited a long time. I can't rush to judgment.*

~

The employee fair for senior students would begin next week, and Mike wanted to take part in searching out just what was out there for him. He had set the materials about his search aside and had not been into them for the past year—not since he'd received the letter from the county clerk in Michigan—although he hadn't forgotten about his investigation, journey, and probe into from where he came. The letter from the county clerk had created a pause, a discouragement.

◉◉

Aaron and Mike had decided to meet the following Wednesday at the same time and place. They both showed up on time.

"How'd your week go?"

"I think I found out what I want to do when I graduate."

"And?"

"I'm interested in working in the prison system."

"Prison! I thought criminology with an investigative approach was your interest."

"It was, but I talked to one of the recruiters from the Bureau of Prisons and the State Department of Corrections. I can make a better income working with them.

"Mike, you're off on a wonderful adventure of a career. I remember when I finished my residency and started to look for a clinic back home. I was so excited. You seem that way now. Life is such an adventure. My wife, Maria, came from Italy, and she has been a joy to me. As I told you before, she had a loss of her first husband. It was tragic and she was injured as well, but survived. I first met her after I settled in Pittsburgh. We saw each other at a meeting several years ago at the Society of Dermatology Associates, SODA they called it, and we met again after her husband died."

"Can I make this be a part of my essay about you?"

"No, this is just a private conversation between us. Please do not include any of what I've just said in your assignment. Let's start where we left off."

"Well, as long as we're just talking and if you're comfortable talking about it, I'd like to ask you more about your personal DNA donations while you were a student at Michigan. My computer is off; my pencil is on the table."

Aaron hesitated, pursed his lips, folded his hands in a prayer position, and placed the index fingers to his mouth and nose. After about thirty seconds, he said, "Sure, as long as this is just a private conversation."

"I'm a man of my word, Aaron, and I promise not to reveal or write anything about it. I promise. I have never been a donor, yet, but I find it intriguing."

"Okay. Go ahead with your questions."

Mike started, "How many of these donations did you do?"

"I did six," Aaron replied. "I did three each during my medical school years, and three at Michigan when I was enrolled in a two-year specialty program. Sure, the money came in handy, but I felt a sense of me being out there and asked myself if I realized what I was doing."

"Did you inquire or want to know if you fathered any children?"

"No, I never wanted to find out if I did. I didn't want to know if my donations had been used. I still don't want to know. I don't want anyone contacting or looking for me. I made it clear there would be no information revealed until after my death." Aaron stopped and looked at Mike. "Why don't we get back to where we left off about my family?"

Mike felt a sinking feeling and became more convinced it made sense to wonder if this is his father. Things were starting to add up. The letter from the county clerk in Michigan had stated he could not know about his mother's donor until after the donor's death. *I'm going to drop it*, he decided.

"Okay," Mike replied, and he turned on his laptop.

"We left off talking about your brother. Can you tell me about your family?"

Aaron started, "When my brother was in elementary school, other parents complained about him being too rough at recess." Aaron continued about his family life, describing how controlling his father was and how cavalier his brother always was.

"Did your father have a lot of control over what went on in your household? Or was it a cooperative affair with all of you?"

"Yes, my father had control over the family, and it was always about my brother."

"Were you angry with your brother and your father spending so much time together without you?"

"Of course I had some feelings about it. I spent my time studying and enjoying the success of good grades. I knew college was in the offing, but my dad always said I'd have to find a way to finance it because they could not afford it. That's where the scholarship came in, as I told you before." Aaron hesitated and Mike sat quietly. "Tell you what, Mike, I need to quit for today. I don't know how to finish this, but let's just put it off for a while. When is your paper due?"

"It has to be in a month before graduation, by May first. We have plenty of time, and you've given me a lot of good information. It'll take some time to put it all together."

Mike and Aaron left. Mike thought, *Maybe I should just let it go for a month or so. Maybe I should just let it go altogether.* Besides, Mike reminded himself, *I have some work to do on my own these next few months.*

28

Fall and winter came, and spring was in the air. The days were getting longer, and Mike was looking forward to graduation and his future work.

It was now March, and the senior year was going by quickly, with Mike set to graduate in June. He'd completed the four-year course in three years, with a GPA of 3.75. He wasn't happy with his GPA because one of his professors, with whom he'd had two classes, never gave a 4.0—ever—and he felt he deserved a 4.0.

After a background check, two interviews with the FBI, and an interview with the Department of Corrections, Mike secured a job with a prison in Ohio, near where he'd grown up. His job would introduce him to the work of admission and orientation. He could not have imagined such success six years ago when he'd started at the naval hospital.

Graduation was June 6, and he would report to his assignment July 15. This gave him plenty of time to pack up, drive up, get a new apartment, unpack, and be ready to go to work.

He continued his work at St. Ben's. The clinic valued him as an important volunteer and honored him at a fundraiser.

One morning, Aaron came in a little late. He apologized to Mike for his arrival time. Mike noticed the index finger of his left hand was wrapped in gauze and a bandage.

"What'd ya do?" Mike asked with a perplexed expression on his face and a serious tone to his voice.

"I was helping Maria this morning. She's making a pot of minestrone and lets it slow cook all day. I was slicing carrots on a mandolin, and I got my finger too close to the blade. You ever do that?"

"I not only haven't done it, I don't even know what a mandolin is, other than a musical instrument."

Aaron laughed and said, "You need to marry an Italian."

"I think I'll work on that." Mike continued, "Come over here. I'm experienced, and your dressing needs changing. It's blood-soaked. I'll take care of it. I had a good teacher."

"Let's do it before we open the door for the guests, or better yet, the patients. I'll be your first patient of the day."

"Good choice. You probably won't be able to use your hand for a while, but I gotcha covered."

Mike opened the dressing on Aaron's finger, and it did not look good. "You really sliced it. Wow! There's a piece of skin here I think needs to come off. It's hanging by a thread."

"Well, go ahead and cut it off. It'll heal."

Mike carefully opened a pack of instruments and some sterile gloves. He put together a bandage and laid out the necessary supplies on a tray. They were all sterile. Aaron said the finger was sore, so Mike cut off the skin, took some Novocaine and Polysporin ointment, and put it on. He redressed the wound, and Aaron said it felt much better. The pain had quieted. Mike cleaned up the tray.

"You're a darn good learner," Aaron said.

"Okay, then. No charge."

Mike took over the clinic that day. Aaron was not able to do much because of the bandage on his finger. It got in the way of everything, including writing. Aaron was not ambidextrous. Mike tried to talk him into going home early, but Aaron toughed it out until noon, the usual closing time.

Mike made sure the bandage was secure before Aaron left and he cleaned up the clinic before leaving.

29

A month later, Mike met Aaron at the coffee shop and told him of his assignment with the Bureau of Prisons.

"Mike, I am so proud of you and where you are going in life." Aaron leaned forward in his chair, a great smile on his face, his head nodding enthusiastically. "We have worked together for two years, and I have to say the pleasure was all mine. I think the best moments of the volunteer job, for you, were your personal satisfaction helping those who needed help."

Mike nodded in agreement, an expression of pure pleasure on his face.

Aaron continued, slowly nodding his head. "I think the saddest moment for us both was when Janet died. Her death was so needless, so sudden, especially because it was a drug overdose." He sighed and seemed to be looking into the far-off distance. "Those are the moments we can't control, and who'd of thought it?" he added softly.

Mike pursed his lips, recalling Janet's face. Her death had, indeed, been difficult to cope with. And he had been thankful for Dr. Ben's guidance during that period when they'd both confronted their grief at her passing.

"I can't tell you what a pleasure it's been to have you working with me," Aaron said, bringing Mike back to the present.

The Day Always Comes

"Thanks, Aaron. I've definitely enjoyed working at St. Ben's. I've met so many people who were down and out, and helping them gave me much satisfaction. It made me realize how fortunate I am.

"I want to stay in touch with you," he added. "Would it be possible for me to have your e-mail address and cell phone number? That is something we have never done between the two of us. I promise to communicate via e-mail. That's easiest. But if I need to get some information 'pronto,' as my mother would say, I would like to call you."

"I think that's a reasonable question. I, too, would like to stay in touch. Also, before you go, I would like to take you to dinner and have you meet Maria."

Mike smiled, "Wow! That would be great. I would love to meet her, and I look forward to it. I accept. Let's check schedules and go from there."

As they rose from the table to leave, Aaron pulled his sunglasses out of his pocket. He also had a baseball cap in his left hand. Just before Aaron got in his car, he put on the cap. It was dark blue with a Detroit Tigers logo on the front. Mike stared for a minute as Aaron put on a pair of Ray-Bans.

"It's him," Mike whispered out loud to himself. "That's the guy I saw at the library three years ago, before I started at St. Ben's. I can't believe it. Three years ago." This was starting to come together, but there were too many missing pieces that still remained undiscovered. Mike wondered again as he had so many times, *Was it him? Is Aaron my father? What was he doing in the section of the library about finding one's parent from a donor or finding offspring? Now I understand. I am 99 percent convinced Aaron is my father, but I can't prove it. I have to find that remaining 1 percent. But how? I don't know, but I will think through this. I will find out.*

Two weeks later, Mike and Aaron had made a date for an evening dinner. Mike was eager to meet Maria. He e-mailed Aaron and said he would be in the bar. Dinner reservations were set for seven. Mike showed up early to have a scotch before Aaron and Maria arrived.

103

A few moments later, Aaron walked in with a strikingly beautiful woman at his side. She had strawberry blond hair done up in a bun in the back and delicately smooth skin. She appeared trim and fit and obviously took good care of herself.

The introductions completed, they settled at a table in the main dining room, which offered a quiet but elegant atmosphere. Aaron knew the maître d', so the service would no doubt be good.

Meeting Maria was fun. Mike had had no idea of her beauty. She seemed shy and maybe slightly introverted. She didn't speak much, but you could tell she was Italian, with a slight but beautiful accent when she did speak.

The evening went well, and Mike and Aaron exchanged conversation about working together. They left, and Mike thanked Aaron for the evening and the pleasure of meeting Maria. Mike drove home with a smile, thinking, *Dad just took me to dinner.*

30

Sunlight appeared through the window of the bedroom, and Mike was up early on the morning of July 15, ready for his orientation. The drive north had been pleasant, with a clear sky and warm temperatures. He had quickly found an apartment and prepared himself for his eight thirty report time. The bureau sent him information about the area of the prison, as well as nearby apartments, condos, townhouses, and high-rise rentals. He wanted to live where it would be convenient for him to get to work. As he became familiar with the city, he could move where he wanted, when he wanted. Immediately on arrival, he searched for and found an apartment.

He received a pass in his welcoming packet in the mail, authorizing his entrance through gate 11. The time was eight. The meeting would begin at eight thirty. He presented the pass with his driver's license. The greeting by the guard seemed officious but seriously pleasant. He walked straight ahead to room 218, following the information he received. There was one other person in the room, also a new hire. A staff person greeted Mike and offered him coffee and a selection of rolls.

"Help yourself," Tom Dillard said, presenting his hand to greet Mike. "You may as well start the day enjoying prison food."

They both smiled, and Mike could sense Tom was an outgoing, gregarious guy with a sense of humor. Mike poured himself a cup, and they engaged in some pleasant conversation.

A moment later, two young women and another man walked into the room. Tom Dillard greeted them, and everyone greeted each other with handshakes and smiles.

"If you have a cup of coffee and a pastry, we can start and even finish early. Help yourself to coffee anytime. Make yourselves comfortable."

Mike took a seat at the end of the row next to a striking young woman. She introduced herself as Carrie O'Leary. This would be her first job. Mike thought, *With her striking looks, it may not be a good place for her first job.* But that wasn't his decision. She must be qualified. She was lean and had strawberry blond hair down to her shoulders and a slim figure. Her speech pattern was typically northern, almost Canadian sounding, and she wore little makeup, but she smelled wonderful.

"Hi, I'm Mike Gibbons," he said. "This is my first employment, or rather my second. The Navy was my first."

"Really," she smiled. "And where are you coming from?"

"I just graduated from a university in Tampa."

"The warm south to the cold north. Have you lived here before?"

"Yes, I grew up in southern Michigan near Ann Arbor, so it's not new to me."

"Then there'll be no surprises, just refreshers."

"How about you? Where are you from? You sound almost Canadian."

Carrie smiled. "You are not the first one to say that to me. My parents are from Canada, so I suppose I picked up a lot of their slang, shall we say, eh?"

There was a moment of silence and a chuckle between them. "I graduated from Indiana University's School of Nursing, with criminology as my minor. I grew up in a small suburb of Bloomington, Indiana, and enrolled at the university right after high school. The small talk was over, and Tom wanted to get right down to business. He invited everyone to individually introduce themselves and tell a little about where they were coming from. Mike repeated what he'd told Carrie.

Tom explained the protocol of entering and exiting, which was always through gate 11, the entrance they'd used that morning. In a few minutes, they would have their pictures taken for their ID cards, receive their parking permits, and then get fingerprinted. The ID cards would be used in all the scanners at the prison. Beginning the next day, they would have to use their ID cards to enter gate 11. Even though an officer on duty may know them in time, without the ID card, they would not be allowed into any area of the prison. The ID card would record their entrance and exit wherever they might go.

There was also plenty of paperwork in a well-organized information packet regarding retirement, pay, and instructions on how to deal with and be careful with the prison population. After lunch, they would go and be fitted with their uniforms—their "work clothes," as Tom Dillard explained. The next day, they would meet with Warden Tony Barba.

The orientation ended early at two thirty. It was a beautiful day, and Mike wanted to go back to his apartment and go for a run before dinner. He wondered if Carrie was a runner. She was slender and looked as if she kept herself in good shape. She appeared to be about the same age as him.

After they had received their ID cards and uniforms, Mike and Carrie walked together toward the exit.

"I bet you're a runner," Mike said with a quizzical look.

"I am, and I plan to go for a run after I get back to my apartment."

"I plan to do the same. Would you care to join me?"

"Oh, that would be great. I'm at 1225 Commerce Street. Are you close?" she asked.

"Hey, I'm right around the corner on Commerce Circle. Why don't you give me a call when you're ready, and I'll pick you up." Mike gave her his phone number. He thought of Mary—déjà vu. When Mike got home, he sent a quick note to Aaron:

> *Hey, Aaron.*
>
> *I arrived safely and already have had a day of orientation. I don't know my assignment yet, but I know I won't be working directly with the general population of inmates right away.*
>
> *One of the new hires with me is a beautiful young woman from Indiana University. We already have a run together planned later today and hopefully dinner after, but I haven't asked her yet. It doesn't take me long. I'll keep in touch and let you know how it all goes.*
>
> *Meanwhile, best to you, and I loved meeting Maria.*
>
> *Mike*

31

The next morning, Mike showed up early. Carrie was already there, and she and Mike again sat next to each other. The coffee tasted fresh and good. Mike had not made any before leaving the apartment. The other two men walked in, and handshakes were in order. The second female entered, and she seemed friendly but distant. They were all wearing their work clothes issued to them the previous day. The greetings were pleasant. Mike decided this was going to be a good experience. He was going to make it that way. So far, he was happy with what he was doing.

"Great run yesterday. I enjoyed it," Carrie started with a sip of her coffee.

"Oh, me too. I've always enjoyed a run in the afternoons before dinner. You may as well know, my mantra is run to eat and eat to run, or eat, or run, but I like to combine the two."

"Oh, and yes, thank you for inviting me out to eat after. Even though it was Culvers, the burger tasted delicious."

"You're welcome! I enjoyed it as well. Culvers is my favorite place, but if we do it again, we may get more formal and go somewhere a step above Culvers."

They both laughed, Mike thinking, *your first date with someone and you take her to Culver's.*

Then, for some strange reason, Mike's thoughts went to the house on Chestnut and Grand where Nancy Moore's murder happened. He felt sad and shook his head slightly. *It must have been the talk about taking a run before dinner.* They both continued to eat a roll and drink their coffee. He remembered always passing Nancy's house.

Tom Dillard walked in with another gentleman. The man with him was of average height and well-dressed. Tom introduced him as Warden Tony Barba.

"Great to have you here," the warden started. He had a gravelly voice and was slightly barrel-chested. Mike knew the symptoms of emphysema and chronic obstructive pulmonary disease (COPD) from smoking, and Warden Barba showed them beautifully. The warden continued, "I want you to know there were many applicants for these four positions, and you were the best of the best. Welcome."

Tony greeted each one individually with a handshake. It was as if he knew each of them well before they arrived. Mike could smell the acrid residue of cigarette smoke as the warden greeted him.

Warden Barba went on to give them an outline of the prison population. Each would receive a mentor to help with their orientation. None would work in direct contact with the prison population until they were up to speed and their training wheels were taken off. He made it clear they would never be alone, and their safety would be the first order of their employment.

"Each of you will receive an assignment in an area of the prison we feel is a fit for you according to your résumé. You will not be in a position you don't like. If you do not want to be in the particular area you are assigned to, and there is another position available, you can apply for it. We want you to enjoy your time here. We don't say the same to the incoming 'residents,' shall we call them."

Everyone laughed at the light humor. The morning meeting ended, and after lunch, they would be meeting with their mentors.

The lunch in the employee dining room went fine, and Mike invited Carrie to a run again. She had some errands to do and thought it best she do them, so they decided on the next day.

The four candidates returned to room 218, and five people, three men, including Tom and two women, were there. Tom Dillard introduced the four new arrivals as their mentors. Mike met Mark Smyth, an older gentleman who had a great smile, a firm handshake, and good eye contact. They went off to their individual assignments to begin the work waiting for them.

Mark was assigned with Mike on the first few admissions. He caught on fast. There was to be no conversation between the incoming inmates and Mike. If they did ask a question, Mike would not answer them, but one of the guards was there to take over.

32

It was hard to imagine a year had passed. Mike moved from his apartment to the twenty-sixth floor of a high-rise closer to the city, in a suburban area where young professionals lived. The view of the city was spectacular, facing west. It had a large balcony with a door to the living room and one at the end to the bedroom. Carrie had helped him find the apartment and had given him some suggestions about interior design. It was the woman's touch Mike needed.

At the prison, Mike had become well-liked by his peers and the other prison staff. He caught on quickly and conducted himself professionally. He never became friendly with any inmate because this would be the only time he would see them. Nor did he act or speak in an abusive or degrading manner to any of them. He saw some inappropriate happenings, but he let the proper prison staff handle those issues.

Mike and Carrie had been dating since they'd met. They both enjoyed each other's company and gave the appearance they were becoming serious about a life together. They went to the movies, athletic events or just took walks around the city. They were together as a couple when either was invited to a party or event. There were designated walks through gardens and biking paths, which they took advantage of, and they just enjoyed being together. They delighted in each other's company.

When Christmas came that year, Carrie asked Mike if he had time off and was going home.

"I am home. Besides, I have to work Christmas morning but only a half day."

"I have never heard you mention your family. Do they live here or are they in southern Michigan?" she asked.

Mike hesitated, realizing he had never told Carrie about his early years. He had told her about growing up in southern Michigan, being in the Navy, and his college years at the university in Tampa. Her question didn't feel like she was nosy, just making general conversation. He thought for a moment, and Carrie could sense the delay in his answer.

"Actually, I have no family," he told her. "My mom died in a car accident when I was four years old. My grandma raised me and lived just north of here, but she died several years ago. So I'm by myself. I've gotten used to it."

Carrie stood with a quiet look on her face. She moved her head slightly and smiled. "Not even brothers or sisters?"

"Not a single one."

"I can't imagine it, and what about your father?"

"I will have to tell you about my family sometime."

"If you had the whole day off, you'd be welcome to come to Indiana at my parents home. We have such a wonderful family gathering."

"Thank you so much. Maybe some other time. That's thoughtful of you to think of me. Why don't we get together tonight, if you want, and I'll tell you about where I came from. It's a long short story. There's no better time than now."

Carrie smiled, nodded, and immediately said, "Yes, of course."

"Good. I'm done at three. I'll pick you up at six thirty. Will that work for you?

"Yes, I finish at five. See you at six thirty."

Mike thought this might be his pass card into attaining something he had thought about many times before—a comparison between

Aaron's genetics and his own. After all, Carrie worked in the clinic with access to medical testing.

Mike completed his day and went home. Although it was mid-December, the weather was in the midfifties, and the sun shined brightly. He decided just to go for a walk and wore only lightweight comfortable clothing. On his return, he showered, changed into some casual clothes, and left his apartment at six fifteen to pick up Carrie. She was still in the original place she'd rented when she'd started working at the prison. Mike went to her side of the car to open the door.

"Hey, great to see you. You look wonderful out of that nurse's uniform."

"Thanks. I wish we could wear just a smock top and be more comfortable. Our workplace is full of rules and regulations, for not only the inmates, but also the employees as well."

"Yes, I know. You have a good point. I reserved a table at Ristorante Italiano for seven. They have great food and a wonderful atmosphere."

"Perfect!" Carrie answered. "I love Italian with a good bottle of red."

They valet parked the car, and after the maître d' had directed them to a table near the window in a quiet area, they started with a scotch for each of them. He loved the fact that she enjoyed scotch. The conversation started light, centering on their workplace. Both were happy to be where they were, and neither had had any problems. This lasted about twenty minutes.

"So tell me," Carrie started. "What's this about your family? I've been so curious since you told me about yourself earlier today."

Mike smiled, hesitated with his elbow on the table and chin in the palm of his hand, took a deep breath, let it out, and took a sip of his scotch. He leaned slightly forward. "Well, here is the story of where I came from. Once upon a time," he started.

There was a moment of light laughter. "You have such a great sense of humor."

Mike began with his conception and the death of his mother. He continued, telling her about his grandmother and how she raised him.

She was his "mom." Carrie listened intently. She knew of artificial insemination and where the donor samples came from and the bank where they stored them, but she had never met anyone who was an offspring of the procedure. Mike told her of his search, his birth certificate, and his correspondence with the county clerk in Michigan. And then he told her about his meeting with Aaron Kelly, better know as Dr. Ben, and how the doctor had finished college and had arrived where he was today.

"Mike, that is an incredible story! I have often wondered about people who come from donors. I can't believe you've gone all these years and not found your father."

"That's the problem. He, whoever he is, left specific instructions to be unknown until six months after his death. In the beginning, I had no interest. My focus on telling you is, I am curious, wondering—almost convinced actually—that Aaron Kelly is my father. He gave six samples while in college. We are so similar. We're both left-handed and have blonde hair and blue eyes. We're the same height, and we have the same interests. Our voices even sound alike."

"That's amazing! Why did you take so long to tell me? And what would you do if you did find out he is your father? Would it satisfy you to leave it the way it is and not let him know you know?"

"Right now, I have no need to meet the donor, even if it is Aaron. I just want to know the answer to the equation; I would know, and it would be the end of the story."

Carrie shook her head from side to side. He could tell she enjoyed the conversation. His thoughts came to reality. *I love her and would like to get into a closer relationship. I would like it if she became Mrs. Mike Gibbons.*

"It's been a curiosity to find out who he is, where he is," he continued. "Is he married? Does he have children by his marriage? Do I have half brothers or half sisters? You see, the questions get bigger and bigger, longer and longer."

The waiter came to see if he could take their order or perhaps bring them an appetizer.

"I think we'll have another scotch," Mike said, "and when you bring them, we'll be ready to order. Is that all right with you, Carrie?"

"Sure. Let's enjoy another round." Carrie leaned forward, her blue eyes sparkling, her feminine smell exciting. "This is an amazing story." She smiled.

They took each other's hands and held them tightly. There was a quiet moment wherein the two of them shared a smile that was just for them, clearly acknowledging the affection that was growing between them. Mike leaned forward, and Carrie met him halfway. They kissed, not lightly, but firmly and briefly so as not to attract attention to their table.

Mike continued. "There is something I would like to ask you." He hesitated. "I don't know because it's another one of those 'I-don't-know-where-to-go-from-here' thoughts."

"Go ahead. You never know until you ask."

"I would love to have you as my wife."

Carrie sat up, smiled, opened her mouth, and said, "Oh, Mike, yes. I would love to be your wife. We've been dating for a year now, and I have enjoyed it immensely."

"Let's work on it and make plans. We can go diamond ring shopping this coming weekend. When you go home for Christmas, you can let the family know, or we can delay it to another time when I can also go. And another thought." Mike smiled and displayed a moment of joy. "I want to ask Aaron to be my best man."

"Oh, Mike! I am so happy. Yes, let's go shopping this weekend. Aaron is a great choice. I will tell my family all about you over Christmas. I love you!"

"And I love you, Carrie! We'll talk about and make plans to visit your family."

They spent the rest of the evening just looking at each other and sharing constant smiles.

33

A few weeks went by, during which time Mike and Carrie shopped for a diamond ring. He wanted a 1.5 carat solitaire, and Carrie thought that was beautiful. A solitaire was exactly what she would choose, but the 1.5 carat wasn't necessary. Mike insisted. He had the money for it from his grandma's inheritance. It was fun being together and making plans for their lives. The walks, runs, football games, movies, and seeing each other at work were all exciting times for both of them. They told no one about the engagement. Carrie wanted to go home Christmas, and she wanted Mike to meet her family before they announced their plans.

One evening, they were together, and Mike looked at Carrie and said, "I have a question for you that has been on my mind for quite some time."

Carrie looked quizzically at Mike and waited for his response.

"Would it be possible to get a deoxyribonucleic acid test done?"

Carrie hesitated, looked at Mike, and said, "You are so funny. Why don't you just say DNA?"

Mike kept smiling. "Well, I wanted to be exact."

Carrie shook her head, and, with a big smile, but a serious look, she turned her head to Mike. "Are you asking me to participate in doing it?"

"Yes, if you can, as long as it's legal."

Carrie stared at Mike but did not respond. She just looked at him and smiled, slowly turning her head from side to side. He could tell the computer in her brain was in the "search mode."

"Well, anything is possible," she started. "I think we could do it at the prison clinic, but all DNA tests have to have the approval of the warden, and furthermore, an attorney or doctor usually requests them. You can't just simply decide you want one. It doesn't work that way. And besides, what is this for?"

"I want a comparison of my DNA and Aaron's. How difficult do you think it would be to get one?"

"I don't know, but I'd bet it would be very difficult."

They both sat quietly for a moment. Carrie looked at Mike and said, "How do you plan to make the comparison? Do you have a sample from Aaron we could use? An article of clothing, a coke can, something he may have used?"

"I have something from him that's better than any of those, and Aaron does not know I have it."

"Can you tell me what it is?"

"Later, if I can get the approval. I'll bring it to you. It'll be a game of show-and-tell."

"Well," Carrie hesitated. "This is not going to be easy, but I'll get to work on it, research what to do and how to handle it, so as not to raise suspicions. I've never done this before, and you know how the talk goes with the prison employees."

"Yes, I do, and you are the only person here who knows about my heritage. If you will, please keep it between us."

"I will, and I'll also get to work on this. But you have to understand that the warden will have to know the reason for my request."

Mike nodded, agreeing.

"I will tell him the entire story when he needs to know. And thank you, Carrie. Please know this request from me will not go unrewarded, even if the warden says no." Mike took Carrie in his arms and kissed her gently. "I love you so much."

34

After about two weeks, Mike met Carrie in the coffee shop.

"I have the DNA test paperwork all completed. When do you want me to give it to Warden Barba?"

"You can do it right away," Mike answered.

"Okay. I'll get on it. But don't get your hopes up. Your request is unusual. I discussed it with one of the doctors without giving him any names. I presented it to him as a curiosity for a paper I said I wanted to write. He told me Tony Barba has only approved a personal request of this nature from an employee twice in his twelve years as warden. I'll let you know as soon as I hear back."

"Fair enough. I'll just wait to hear."

"Good idea," Carrie replied.

Mike went on about his work in the admission and orientation section of the prison. He hadn't heard from Carrie about the DNA test, and three weeks had passed. Each time they saw each other at lunch or anywhere in the building, she would not mention anything about it, except to shake her head no. Mike felt he should exercise caution and told himself; the answer would come when it was ready to come. After all, it had been a long time already. He decided he'd be patient.

Tony Barba approached Mike at lunchtime and asked if he would come to his office later in the day. Mike agreed and said he'd finish about three. Thoughts started racing through his head. *This has to be the DNA request*, he told himself. *Or, maybe it isn't. I hope I'm not in trouble because of my request. I can't think of anything I've done. I always do my job. What could this be about?* Mike decided that, if the DNA test was, in fact the reason he'd been summoned, the warden would probably want to know why he'd made the request. He was prepared to explain. And he was determined that, whatever the warden's answer—be it an approval or a rejection—he would accept it.

For the rest of the day, Mike was on pins and needles and could not get the meeting off his mind. In fact, his mind was running like crazy. Six new prisoners were arriving at one-thirty, and he would have to take care of their admission and orientation. He would finish his day's work shortly before three and then go straight to the warden's office.

The six prisoners arrived at about one twenty, and the admissions began. He recognized one young man. The young man recognized Mike. He immediately realized this was the young kid who'd tried to steal his car when he was in Tampa. But how had he gotten to Ohio? His paperwork stated he was in for armed robbery and car theft; twenty-five years might straighten him out. The young man attempted to strike up a conversation with Mike, but one of the guards put a stop to it immediately.

"One more word out of you and you're toast," the guard said to the young man. "Shut your mouth! You don't talk to anyone unless we tell you to do so. You're gonna be here for a long time. Don't start off on the wrong foot."

Mike said nothing except what he told each inmate entering the prison.

Round and round his mind went all afternoon. Finally, the time of the meeting approached. He finished his duties, climbed the stairs, and walked into Warden Barba's office on the third floor. He liked the stair exercise.

He walked in, and the secretary recognized him. "Go right in. He's expecting you."

The Day Always Comes

Mike decided to take in a few deep breaths. He needed to calm down. It didn't matter what the warden wanted; it was already determined. He would just have to listen. The door was open; Mike knocked and entered the office.

Tony Barba stood up and greeted him with a firm handshake and a smile.

"Wow," the warden said. "Good firm handshake. You must lift."

"I was a wrestler in high school, did some intramural events in college, and helped out at a high school in Tampa while in college. I intend to stay in shape."

"Well, it's good to have you here, Mike. I've heard excellent feedback, and I also understand you have a background in medicine. I got that from your application."

"Yes. I helped at a clinic in Tampa for the homeless when I was in college. There was a doctor who came twice a week to help them, and I assisted him. He taught me how to work with the homeless, medically, physically, and emotionally."

"I'm going to cut to the chase as to why I have asked you to my office. We're going to have an opening that we think would fit you. With your background and knowledge, I, and the advisory committee think you'd be perfect for the job. You will train for the next few months and then take over when the present staff member retires."

"I'm open to anything, and if it means advancement for me, I'm willing to give it a try. May I ask more about it now?"

Tony Barba sat back in his chair and clasped his hands together. He coughed. "It would be preparing the items for lethal injection to carry out the sentence of a prisoner on death row."

Mike was speechless for a few moments. Warden Barba had put it straight to him without hesitation.

Tony continued. "You would not be responsible for ending a person's life. It's the state who ends it. Two prison guards would be with you as you prepare the lethal injection drugs. You would never be alone. This event is carrying out a sentence that is, as I said, set by the state."

Mike sat with his eyes looking down at his knees. He didn't speak, and the warden didn't either. Mike took in a deep breath, cocked his head to the side, smiled and said, "What prompted you to select me?"

"Mark Smyth, the man who gave you the orientation. That is the work he has been doing for about ten years."

Mike sat remembering Mark, but he had not seen him since.

"Can I have time to think about this, say until tomorrow after my workday? I don't intend to discuss this with anyone. It will be my decision."

"You may take the time you want. Mark is retiring in six months. The preparation time would allow you the training period, and then you'd take over the work yourself. You will have plenty of time in between those events to work with Mark if any questions or concerns arise. We have a couple of executions coming up in the next four months. It would be a good time for you to start, but I would have to know within a couple of days. You'll remain in your job as an admission officer and perform these duties as an extra event. Besides, it will be a pay raise for you of five hundred dollars per month."

Mike sat pensively. He looked at the warden and said, "Thank you for considering me for this position. I will take the next twenty-four hours to think about it, and I'll see you tomorrow. Is that okay with you?"

"Perfect. I look forward to your answer, and whatever it is, it's your decision."

Mike and the warden stood up, shook hands again, and Mike left. Walking down the hall to the stairs, he could hear the warden coughing in a deep, guttural hack. As he drove home, his mind was spinning.

Then he thought of a plan. This offer could be a game of give and take. He smiled. *A quick run to clear my mind, listen to a tape, and I should have my game plan in place.*

35

Mike thought carefully about what he would say to the warden the next day. The conversation could be a turning point for him in his career, but it could also be an answer to the DNA question. He arrived at work early, as usual, and had a cup of coffee and a roll.

Just as he sat down, Carrie came into the cafeteria. She looked at Mike and shook her head no, meaning no response from the warden.

Mike motioned to her to sit with him. She picked up her coffee and came to his table.

"Good morning," Carrie said.

"Good morning to you," Mike replied.

"You have a sunshine face this morning. Have I ever said how dashing you look in your prison clothes?"

"I know, I've said you look professional in your nurse's costume, but you've never complimented me on my work clothes."

They both grinned at each other, but Mike looked at Carrie with a devilish smile.

"I see the warden today at three. He wants me to do an extra job."

"Well, your name is out there, if it comes directly from Barba. Maybe it has something to do with the DNA test?"

"I'll tell you all about it. Call me after work. Let's go for a walk by the river and maybe dinner tonight?"

Carrie smiled. "Of course. What time?"

"It'll be at my place if it's okay with you."

Carrie gave a raised eyebrow look and repeated, "What time?"

"I'll pick you up at six, and we'll head for the river walk. Is that good?"

"I'll make it good. I've gotta get to work. See you then."

Carrie stood up, turned, and headed for the door.

Mike sat getting his thoughts together. *This plan should be fun. I like negotiations.*

The day was busy, but included no new admissions. He caught up with some office work he had put aside and decided to get ready for tomorrow. Seven new ones would be coming in. Sometimes Mike had a heavy heart for some prisoners, and yet he could see why some were there, and he never made it his business to have any compassion for them.

He finished his day's work and headed to see Tony Barba. Again, the secretary ushered Mike into the warden's office.

The warden was obviously expecting him and greeted Mike with a slight smile and a hopeful expression. "Well?"

Mike looked at the warden, smiled, hesitated, and said, "I accept."

The warden grinned, stood up, and shook Mike's hand. He wheezed, took a deep breath, and coughed, turning his head toward the window. "Damn cigarettes. I should have quit before I started. Now I'm paying the price for each pack I bought."

Mike said nothing.

"Somehow, I knew you would. We'll get you started next week with training. You and Mark, who's currently in charge of the setup, will meet for an orientation session. He's retiring after thirty-five years of service, ten at the death house. He started out with a job similar to the one you're doing right now. When I asked him for possible replacement names, your name was the only one given. Everything will be ready for your training, and we'll get you going right away. Your decision is great!"

"Well, I look forward to the new position. I look forward to working with Mark again. However, I have a request," Mike added.

The warden stopped and cocked his head quizzically. "Yes, of course. Go ahead."

"Several months ago, Carrie O'Leary, a nurse in health care services, filed a request for a DNA test, which had to receive your approval for it to go forward. It would be a test I'm seeking for personal reasons, and we have not heard from you about a decision. I wonder if we could include it in the 'I will do for you, and you will do for me' column?"

"I remember it well. However, we don't just do DNA tests because a person wants one. I probably should have had you come to the office then and state your reason."

"I would have," Mike replied. "I didn't know the protocol, and I probably should have researched it before I presented the request."

The warden put his four fingers of his left hand to his forehead and his thumb on his cheek. He closed his eyes and took in a deep breath and coughed. "So where do we go from here?" he asked Mike.

"I don't know, Warden. The ball is in your court."

"Tell me about what you want and why you want it," Tony Barba said.

Mike smiled. "My conception was through artificial insemination. When I was four years old …" And he told the story he'd recited first to Mary and then to Carrie. He knew it well, as it had been on a tape recording in his mind, and he had played it over and over. Speaking clearly, he was careful to include details. This moment was his only chance to move forward. He knew whatever he said would either get him a "go-ahead" or a "denial." He took about twelve minutes to get the story out, and he sensed the warden listened carefully.

When Mike finished, the warden asked him only one question. "This is fascinating, Mike. What do you plan to do with this DNA evidence once the test is completed? If it proves Aaron is not your father, will you drop the issue?"

"I haven't thought that far, but with a little time, I could come up with the answer for you. My first thought is, I would destroy the DNA report."

The warden looked at Mike, gave him a smile, and said, "I will take this into consideration. Can you give me twenty-four hours like I gave you?"

"Yes, I will. In the meantime, I'll accept the work you wish me to do. Your decision will not change my mind about my new position. However, please understand the DNA results are something I want and need to know."

"I'll see you tomorrow at this time."

Mike stood up, extended his hand, and gave a smile of satisfaction.

"Thank you for listening to me, Warden. I'll see you tomorrow."

Tony Barba stood up and extended his hand to Mike. "Yes, you will, and I look forward to your success in your new job. You're going to do just fine."

As Mike left the office, walking down the hall, he could hear the warden coughing.

36

"Welcome. I believe a libation is in order."

"I never thought you'd ask," Carrie replied, turning to Mike with a smile.

"Scotch and water?"

"Just a splash. I don't want to destroy the flavor of the scotch."

"Would you like a martini olive in your drink. I like one, which makes it a faux Rob Roy."

"I've never have had one, but I do like a Rob Roy. Let me try it."

Mike went to the kitchen where he had all the necessary items ready. He always bought bottled water for the scotch instead of using water straight from the tap. He prepared the drinks and took them outside with some Stilton and tapenade.

"Cheers. I love your being at my side and to have you here." Mike raised his glass to clink with Carrie's.

"Thank you. It's good to be here, and I love being here. It's beautiful. I love this area, this building, this apartment. It just needs a feminine touch."

Mike raised his head and chin and gave Carrie a big smile.

"But, more important, first things first. What do you have to tell me? You said you had a couple of appointments with Warden Barba. Are you at liberty to tell me about them?"

"Yes, I am. You and I are the only ones to know this, so here goes."

Mike confided in Carrie the whole story about how the warden had approached him. He'd had no idea about the position of setting up for the execution procedure opening up. He'd never even known the position existed. It hadn't occurred to him that someone had to do it. The inmates on death row arrived at a different location at the prison, and he had no contact with any of them. He felt pleased the warden had asked him.

Mike talked for some time, carefully and methodically laying out the information. Carrie sat, spellbound by what Mike was saying.

"Does it bother you, the idea of being in the position of contributing to the end of a person's life?"

"That's a great question, and I've thought about it. I presented it to the warden when I saw him the first time. He assured me I was doing what the laws of the state dictated. He made it clear I would only do the setup. I would not be the executioner. I would not take part in injecting the drugs. I would be there when the condemned died, but once I'd completed the setup, and the execution was completed, I would clean up and then be free to go. I asked for some time to think about it and told him I would let him know in twenty-four hours. I did."

"You certainly used the word 'I' quite a bit. You must have pondered the decision carefully. And?"

Mike sat, wondering how Carrie would react when he told her the answer. About ten seconds later, he raised his head and looked straight at her. "I accepted the position." He hesitated.

Carrie sat still, took a sip of her drink, and Mike knew she was in deep thought. What she would say concerned him.

"However, there was something I wanted in return," Mike continued.

"Yes, go on. You've opened the door. Now let me in."

"The DNA test."

Carrie again sat quietly for a minute. She finished her scotch, looked at Mike, and smiled. "This is getting good. May I have another scotch? This first one was delicious. What brand is it?"

"It's Bank Note. I bought it to try, and I do like it."

"So do I. I must look for it. Oh, and I liked the olive."

What was she thinking? Mike wondered. She didn't respond to his telling her of his decision. Maybe she needed a little more time to digest it all. Or did she just want to change the subject?

Mike took Carrie's glass and went to the kitchen. He looked out at her and could tell she was in pensive thought, with chin in hand. He was glad to be able to talk to her. She was his contact, and he needed someone to hear him out. She was not a discouraging conversationalist. She was a wonderful listener and a rational thinker. Mike brought the drinks back outside and sat down.

"Thank you." Carrie smiled at Mike, taking her drink. "You told me earlier you had something of Aaron's that could be used for the DNA analysis. Would you tell me what it is?"

Mike reflected on her question and the implications of sharing with her. Was this the right time? He decided it was time for show-and-tell. "Better than that, I will show you."

Mike stood up, put his drink down, and walked to the bedroom. He closed the door, the blinds, and the door to the balcony. He pulled out the bottom drawer of the chest he'd bought while in college and removed the articles of clothing from the bottom drawer. Picking up his shaving kit from the bathroom, he put it on the bedside stand. He entered the four-digit code, which was the last four digits of his social security number, and the false bottom unlocked. He removed it and placed it on the bed, reached in and took out the metal box, and opened it with the key from his shaving kit. Reaching in, he removed a small package and placed it on the bedside stand next to the shaving kit. Touching the other item in the box gave him a sad feeling. He said, "I'm sorry," and closed the lid.

After he had locked the metal box with the key, he put it back in the bottom of the drawer and returned the key to his shaving kit. He turned, picked up the false bottom piece, put it back in place, and re-entered the code on the remote. He listened for the slight hum of it locking in place and then put his clothes on top. He put the drawer back in place and returned to the balcony.

Carrie looked up and didn't see what Mike had in his hand. He sat down and hesitated for a moment, still wondering if this was the right time. He slowly opened his left palm and presented the package.

Carrie stared at it with a straight face, took it, looked it over carefully, and raised her head to Mike with her mouth slightly open.

"This is from Aaron?"

"Yes, it is."

"Where in the world did you get this? How did you get this?"

"One morning when I assisted at St. Ben's, Aaron came in with the index finger of his left hand bandaged. He had cut it on a mandolin slicer as he helped his wife make minestrone. The dressing needed changing, so I took it off, washed the cut carefully, put some ointment on it, and redressed it. There was a piece of skin hanging from the cut. We both decided it should come off, so I removed it. When I finished, he turned to go to the door, which gave me time to wrap the bandage and skin together and put it in a sterile bag. I put the package in my pocket. It has never been opened, and I consider it to still be sterile. I cleaned up the items for disposal and put the contaminated instruments in the tray for sterilization."

As Carrie viewed the bag and its contents, a smile crossed her face. She looked up at Mike and slowly shook her head from side to side. The ziplock sterile bag contained the blood-dried bandage and the piece of skin from Aaron's finger. "You rascal, you! How clever. Can I ask what you were thinking at the time you did this? Did you have a future thought of what you were going to do with it?"

"No, I didn't. I had no idea of what I would do with it. I just did it thinking it might come in handy someday, and I think it has.

"I am astounded, Mike. This is why you would be so good at criminal investigations. You are such a good thinker!"

They both smiled and looked at each other for what seemed a long time. The eye contact, in combination with the fact that Carrie had expressed her obvious acceptance of the effort he'd made years ago, made Mike's body stir with excitement. They stood up, embraced, and gave each other a long, passionate kiss.

He decided to get on with dinner. They went inside, Mike following Carrie. She took her drink; he took his. He grabbed the cheese and cracker tray on the way, just happening to notice how nicely her jeans fit.

As Mike prepared the steaks for grilling, Carrie started the water for the asparagus and took out the knife and cutting board for slicing the mushrooms.

"Be careful with the slicer. I would be forced to retrieve some of your DNA while treating your wound—just in case."

Carrie shook her head, a big smile on her face. "You are something else. I am so proud of you."

Carrie put down the knife, went over to Mike, and put her arms around him, intending to give him a big hug. Their eyes locked onto each other; their lips came together. They could feel the easing of their muscles.

"Shall we relax for a bit before dinner? Mike said.

"I would love to," Carrie said.

37

"Oh, what a beautiful morning, Oh, what a beautiful ..." Mike sang to himself as he left his apartment for work. His thoughts were about the meeting scheduled this afternoon with Warden Barba. This talk would answer the question he'd been wondering about for quite a while now. Once he'd met with the warden he'd know for sure—his plans were either a go or a no-go. Either way, Mike decided this would be the answer to his journey moving forward or reaching a dead end.

The drive, with the CD player on, gave him time to listen to a part of his meditation. It gave him energy for the day's work. He didn't know how many new arrivals he would have, but it didn't matter. Then he remembered; seven new ones had been scheduled for today. He was so excited about the night before, he'd momentarily lost track. After a fun evening, and a late dinner, Mike had taken Carrie to her apartment, as she had to be in early the next morning.

He would admit the seven, performing his duties as he did on any other day. Sometimes it would be as many as twelve, and other times he would "meet and greet" just one. One day, there had been fifteen. He treated the new arrivals all the same. It was the guards who bellowed out the orders.

There were just a few people in the cafeteria. Mike greeted them, and they greeted him. He poured his coffee, grabbed a muffin, and sat down with the morning paper. He had forty minutes to spare before

The Day Always Comes

reporting to his workspace. Carrie came in a few minutes later. He did not see her, as he was reading a part of the paper.

"Good morning, sunshine," Carrie said, greeting Mike with a smile. "I had a wonderful time last night."

Mike looked up from his paper with a smile.

Carrie continued, "You are a gracious host. Good scotch, good hors d'oeuvres, great steak done to perfection, not to mention the asparagus and mushrooms I prepared. But the best of the evening was the appetizer before."

Mike smiled and put down his newspaper. Slowly, he nodded his head up and down. "Carrie, it was a pleasure to have you at my home. You are a wonderful addition to my life. I am enjoying discussing our wedding plans. I am enjoying it immensely, every moment of it. I feel so lucky to have found you and to have you listen to my life story. Thank you."

"You're welcome, and I got to thinking."

"Uh-oh," Mike responded.

"Why don't you come to the clinic? I will do a blood draw; put the vial, along with the bandage from Aaron in a sealed evidence box with my name on it, and place it in a locked drawer. That way, it will all be together, and no one else will have access to it."

Mike thought for a moment. "Maybe that's a good idea. I can bring the bandage in tomorrow. When would you want to do the blood draw?"

"We could do it now. I had to be here at seven and neither of us has to be on duty for another thirty minutes, and it's only me at the clinic until eight thirty."

"Okay. Let's go. If anyone asks about the bandage on my arm, I can just say I had a cholesterol check this morning at my doctor's office."

"Perfect. You always think ahead. I like that."

"Gotta keep the scan moving just like an airline pilot," Mike said, folding up the paper and getting up from the table. He took his coffee with him.

Carrie and Mike went to the third-floor clinic. There they found one woman who worked all night and was eager to go home. She greeted them and asked if she could leave earlier than usual. Carrie gave her the go-ahead, and she packed her bag and left. Carrie prepared the items for the blood draw. Mike sat down in the chair designed for that purpose. It had slots and straps when inmates came into the clinic to have blood taken.

"Should I strap myself in?"

"You're a big guy, and you won't be a problem. But at the press of a button, I'll have five guards on top of you in a flash."

"Okay. I promise to behave myself. Say! We could sure use this at my apartment."

Carrie only smiled and shook her head. She drew the blood, and the vial filled. She held the cotton over the penetration point of the needle and told Mike to hold it while she wrapped a gauze dressing around his arm. She placed the vial in an evidence box with her name clearly written on it.

"Bring me the bandage specimen tomorrow, and I'll put it all together and place it in a drawer in the storage room designed for security purposes. With my name on it, no one will touch it."

Mike, who had on a short-sleeved shirt, got up and gave her a hard kiss and a smile. "Thanks, Carrie. I'll see you in the morning in the cafeteria. I'll have the bandage, and you have yourself a great day. You're a delightful woman. I have my lunch hour from noon to one. Maybe I'll see you there."

"It all depends on my helper, but I'll keep it in mind, you rascal. Now I know I'm right. You're always thinking ahead."

"Yup."

Mike left, and Carrie started on her routine for the day.

38

The new arrivals bus pulled into the gated area of the prison. Mike took his position in the arrival hall. The guards were shouting out orders to the inmates as they exited the bus. It reminded Mike of the TSA personnel when going through security at the airport. Passengers may not think of it in the same way, but Mike heard it at work, and it sounded just the same. The TSA suddenly had power over you. If any new arrival opened his or her mouth or became uncooperative, the guards immediately had their number, and in an instant, they get special treatment.

Mike took a break at ten thirty and went to the cafeteria for a cup of coffee. It was a change from the noise and commotion at the entrance hall. He went over to a computer, which was available to the employees. He usually checked his e-mail when he went home, but he was alone and decided to do it then.

There was one from Aaron.

> *Mike*
>
> *Thanks for all the emails you have sent. I am glad you are doing well. Your new add-on position, well, I won't comment on it. It is your choice and your decision. I will say, however, you are on your way up. Congrats!*
>
> *Sorry to report we had to put the dog down this past*

week. It was a troubling and sad time for both Maria and me. On the same note, I have not been feeling well lately, fatigued and no appetite, plus plumbing problems. Don't worry; they're not going to put me down. Being a doctor, of course, we think we know it all.

I finally broke down and went to my doctor. I have prostate cancer. The type I have is past curable and fast acting. It has already spread to my bones. One year is all they are giving me. I've presented so many of my patients bad news about melanomas, and now, the bad news is for me. It was hard to hear, and a month has gone by already since I saw the doctor.

I'm okay. I've accepted it now. Maria and I are getting our act together. I will write later when maybe I have better news.

Best, as always,

Aaron

Mike stood and reread the email. A look came over him. He glanced down and closed his eyes momentarily, shaking his head from side to side, like he was saying it was not true, saying no. Then he read the email again, a third time. *This can't be happening,* he thought, *but it is.* Throughout his life so far, Mike had faced many unexpected events. His plan to ask Aaron to be his best man at the wedding was now destroyed. *Carrie and I haven't planned on a date, but there was no other person besides Aaron, who I wanted to ask to be my best man.*

He closed the email and decided to think about his response. He had to get back to work. He would, of course, try to go to Tampa to see Aaron before he went, and the sooner, the better. But just then, he thought of taking Carrie with him.

The Day Always Comes

He finished his work of checking in the new inmates, and by then, it was lunchtime. He went through the cafeteria line and saw Carrie sitting by herself. He went up to her and asked to join her.

A grin crossed her face. "Of course, if you behave."

"You bet I will, for now. No, I promise. I will." Mike placed his tray on the table, sat down, and folded the napkin on his lap. "Please, I didn't mean to offend you by my giving you a kiss this morning, I shouldn't have done it in the workplace or made that wisecrack about the chair. I apologize."

"Oh, forget it. You did it in jest; it was funny. You're on your own. Besides, I enjoyed the kiss."

It broke the ice and the silence, and all seemed well. Mike told the news to Carrie about Aaron, and she shook her head, a sad expression crossing her face.

"From what you have said, I think you were fond of him."

"I was and am. Aaron's death will be the second I've experienced since leaving the Navy. The first was a woman I met at St. Ben's and took care of at the clinic. I took care of her feet every day. She died of an overdose of heroin; so sad. Someday I'll tell you her story."

Carrie sat, sensing the sadness coming over him.

"I do want to go and see him, and soon if I can. Would you be willing to go with me? Aaron and I worked closely and well together. He is a great guy and did much good for the homeless people. I see the warden this afternoon, and I'll let him know about it. I will, of course, run this by my supervisor without him knowing I told the warden first. You know how sensitive people are about their territory."

"Oh yes." Carrie stood and put her dishes on her tray and cleaned up where she'd been sitting. "I have to go, but let me know how it turns out with your meeting."

"Will do. Later. Dinner again soon? I love our dinners together. Eat and run, run and eat. It's fun."

Before Carrie left, she looked at Mike with a smile on her face. "Sure. Dinner and dessert, but without the chair."

They both shook their heads and smiled.

It was now two thirty, and Mike's desk area was cleaned up. He walked the hall and took the stairs to go to the warden's office. Entering the reception room, the door to Warden Bagra's office was closed. The secretary greeted Mike and advised him the warden would be out of the office until next week.

"Did he leave any message for me?"

She looked through her paperwork and said, "No, I have none for you. He's meeting with the governor about an execution in a few months. Do you want me to leave a message for him?"

"Oh ... No, that's okay. I'll contact him next week."

He left with his head down, his eyes watching his feet with each step, disappointed he couldn't hear the warden coughing.

He drove home.

39

Mike changed and went for his usual run. He felt better, but remained saddened by the news from Aaron and disappointed the warden hadn't been there. He'd been looking forward to their meeting. *It's so typical of expectations*, he thought. *The greatest plans are always somehow interrupted. We want everything right now. If we don't get it, we constantly think about it, like a helicopter in our minds.*

Back at the apartment, he showered, cleaned up, put on fresh clothes and decided to sit down and listen to one of his tapes. The chair was comfortable. He always went to it when times were irritating and difficult for him. Mike slammed his fists on the armchair and let out a loud moan. He was angry and had not expressed this anger inside for some time. The topic on the tape was "disappointment."

During the session, an idea came to his mind. He put his hand to his face with his index finger on his nose and lips. His eyes moved from side to side and a slight smile came to his face. *Right on*, he thought; he'd found a solution to his knowing if Aaron was his father. *I know he is*, he said to himself. But I have to have it verified in writing.

He put the tape away and thought more pensively. He pondered his past and recalled the incident—the wrongdoing—that had haunted him. *Everyone does something in life that they regret. I certainly did and do.* But this new thought resonated well with him. *Yes, I think it will work and more cleanly than having the DNA test done.* He decided to write a message to the warden and tell him he would no longer be seeking the DNA test. He picked up his phone and left a message on Carrie's voice mail.

"Hey, Nurse Cratchet! How about a quick walk and talk, followed by a bite to eat tonight? I promise to behave. I think I've found a solution to my years of search. I want to share it with you. Lemme know."

He went to his computer and typed a note to the warden, thanking him for considering his request. He said he believed he had found a way to find the answer to the search for his father. The DNA test would not be necessary, and he would no longer continue to request it.

Carrie called back within a half hour. "Mike, I would love to go. Your voice in your voice mail sounded exciting. What in the world do you have in mind to solve your … equation, shall we say?"

"I think you will be amazed, and again, I am always thinking ahead."

"You certainly are. Sorry I didn't get the chair delivered. I needed it today. I'll call you about ten minutes before I am ready." There was a chuckle from both of them and they hung up. Mike looked forward—not only to the meeting with Carrie but ahead to what he hoped would come. *The day always comes*, he thought. Now *everything is starting to fall into place.*

He sat thinking and laughed about the chair. His excitement was making him feel the best he had in a long time. He was certain this would be the solution to his expedition, the chases, his pursuits, or whatever he thought to call it. In fact, he was so excited about it, he fixed himself a scotch and water. "Yes. Yes, yes," he said out loud. It would be about an hour and a half before he picked up Carrie, so a celebratory libation was in order. He wanted to relax and think.

At five of six, his phone rang, and it was Carrie. She was ready. Mike jumped into his Pilot and headed over to pick her up. She was waiting at the street when Mike pulled up. Carrie helped herself to the door and jumped in.

"What's up suddenly?" she asked.

"I have a solution that will not include the DNA test. I will not be bringing Aaron's bandage to you."

"Okay. I'm eager to hear about it. So where are we going?"

"How about we skip the walk and head to Dino's? It's a great place, with a full bar. Given that we both like Italian and you haven't been there yet, I'm anxious to get there early to get a good table. I think you'll like the place."

"Sounds good to me."

Carrie looked over at Mike. He had a grin on his face. "You sound so excited."

"I am, and you'll hear all about it. I can't wait to tell you my plan."

The drive to Dino's was pleasant, spent mostly discussing the day's work. Carrie said she had some compassion for some inmates, as they ended up coming to the clinic when they were sicker than they should be, just because the guards thought they were faking it. One man came with an upper respiratory infection and had complained about it for three days prior. Mike said he didn't talk with any of the arrivals. He just processed them, as required, gave them their handbooks, and let the guards do the rest.

"So what's the big news?" Carrie asked.

"You just hold on. We'll have a scotch and move from there," Mike replied with an upbeat tone, looking briefly at Carrie with a smile on his face.

Carrie looked over at Mike and realized this must be big. She couldn't imagine what solution Mike could have come up with.

Dino's was moderately busy, but they had no problem getting a table. The server came quickly with water and the menus. Two scotches were in order—on the rocks with a twist of lemon.

"Let's take a look at the menu and decide what we want before we get into the conversation."

"Good idea. It'll make the meal flow more smoothly," Carrie added.

The server came and started telling them about the specials that evening. Mike put up his left hand, palm facing the server. "Please don't be offended. We already know what we want. I just want to spare you the epistle." Mike never liked the lingo of reduction sauce or condiments, and all the other adjectives they use to describe meat loaf and its preparation. Mike said he would flag him to bring another round of scotch and then he could put in the orders.

The server smiled and said, "I'm not offended at all. I sometimes wish the restaurant would publish the specials and put them on the tables. It would be so much easier. I'll put in the drink order, and I'll check with you after your next round for your dinner order."

"Thanks very much," Mike said as the server turned and walked to the bar.

Mike looked at Carrie and said, "If the server says, 'and my favorite is,' I don't order it."

"Mike you are so funny. I love your quick sense of humor."

In less than a minute, the server came with the scotch. They clinked their glasses.

"Okay. Here we go," Mike started.

Carrie had a smile of curiosity on her face and sat up, placing her elbows on the table and her chin in her palm.

"When I started my search, I sent the proper forms, as directed, to the county seat in Michigan, where my mother gave birth to me. I received a response about a month later stating they had found the donor of record. He had left specific instructions requesting his name remain sealed and undisclosed until six months after his death. Aaron is now facing death. Six months after he dies, I should, if he is my father, receive a letter from the county seat telling me he is my biological father. As I've said before, I don't know for sure, but I believe he is."

"Oh ... my ... God ... Mike. You are quite a thinker. I am so happy for you and how this is turning out. I just hope this path you're taking doesn't disappoint you. You have your expectations so high, and to have it crashing down on you would be tragic."

"I have thought about it. I think I'm more excited about where it's all going. I go back to the Irish proverb, 'The longest journey begins with the first step.' Or something like that." I realize all the steps I have in my back pocket so far are true to what it says. These and those, this and that, all the detours, side roads, one-ways, but no dead ends, so far."

The server came with the second round of scotch, and Mike placed the food order. Both decided to have the Chilean sea bass with roasted vegetables on a bed of risotto.

The server said, "Good choice," and left.

"Good choice. Everything would have been a 'good choice.' I wonder if it's 'his favorite'?"

Carrie laughed and took a sip of her scotch. "I'm so happy to be here and to see and hear your excitement about your plan to have the search finally settled. I assume I'm the first to hear about your news."

"Yes, you, are! Only three people in my present life know about my past. Me, you, and Warden Barba. I asked him to keep it between the two us. He assured me he would. I don't want it to get out into the workplace. I haven't told him about this new plan and probably won't. All he will know is, I don't want the DNA test any longer. I sent him an e-mail canceling the request. I plan to keep the secret between the three of us and my plan I just described between the two of us."

"You have my word, Mike. I will tell no one."

The entrées came, and both Carrie and Mike thought the sea bass on a bed of risotto was delicious. General conversation filled up the rest of the evening. They talked about the wedding and their life ahead. Mike did not want to dominate a delightful meal with his plan. He thought that would be like asking someone how they were and ending up getting an organ recital. The dinner and being together was so pleasant Mike hated to have it end. But they both had to be at work early the next morning.

"Why don't you stay at my place tonight?"

"Mike, I can't. It's late, and everything I have to get ready for work is at my place. But thanks for the invitation. Maybe sometime soon."

So he drove Carrie home. A long, passionate kiss ended the evening.

40

Two weeks went by, and Mark Smyth, Mike's mentor when he first began his employment, met up with him. Just as Mike remembered, Mark was a pleasant man, tall with graying hair, and he was all business. They sat down to discuss the procedures he would hand over. Two weeks had passed since Mike had told the warden he didn't want the DNA test. There had been no response from Warden Barba.

"This was a good career," Mark started. "But I'm looking forward to retirement."

"Any plans?" Mike asked. "Travel? Golf? Cabin?"

Mark smiled and looked at Mike, "None of the above. Just paper or plastic?"

Mike smirked shaking his head letting out a short stream of breath. He liked the humor and felt he and Mark would get along just fine as they had before. He'd enjoyed being with him during orientation.

"Gotta tell ya, Mike, I got up the other day and looked in the mirror. There were wrinkles on my eyelids." Mike smiled, and Mark continued, "So I shaved, showered, put on clean clothes, and sat down on the edge of the bed. I was taking the wrinkles out of my socks when I suddenly realized I didn't have any on."

Mike burst out with a hearty guttural laugh.

Mark said, "It's time for me to retire, so let's get on with your orientation."

Mike sat up, still with a smile, and became attentive.

"You will do the setup to the procedure for injection into the subject. You are not the executioner. Remember this—you are not the executioner." Mark was emphatic, pointing his finger at Mike.

"Subject?" Mike asked.

"Yes, we refer to the condemned as 'the subject.' After the attending medical staff person pronounces, you will also clean up, destroy the syringes used, and lock up, all of which I will explain as we go. Then you will sign out, and you will be free to go. No paperwork needed. I'll go over the entire procedure with you. Let's go over to the building where this all takes place."

Mark and Mike walked over to Building 21, better known as simply "21," death row. Mike had never been in 21 before. He'd never even been near it. The day was warm, the sky clear, and Mike still wondered what he was getting himself into. They entered the building, paused, walked up to a cell door, swiped their ID cards, and waited for the door to open. Once inside, the door they'd entered through closed behind them. They stood before a one-way glass shaped like the ticket window at a theater. A door slid open electronically, they proceeded forward, and it closed behind them.

"Wow, 21 really has a secure entrance," Mike remarked.

"This is probably the most secure building at the prison," Mark answered.

The officers inside, who were seated at a desk, knew Mark. They had never seen Mike.

"This is my replacement," Mark said. "Meet Mike Gibbons."

The officers shook hands with Mike, greeting him pleasantly. They smiled and seemed officious. Mike sensed they were sizing him up. The interior of the building appeared cold, plain, drab, and eerily quiet. There was no conversation, and the officers began explaining in detail the procedure for entering.

One of the officers started, "You will always come through this door. Scan your ID to enter, and scan it when you leave. Two of us will unlock the door to the room where the execution takes place. The keys to the room are in a separate drawer in the cabinet over there." The guard pointed to a small cabinet in the corner of the room. "The chemicals used are in a separate room and cabinet. The rules dictate you need two separate keys. The senior guard on duty has one key to the drawer. You, Mike, will have the other. A guard will always be with you from the moment you arrive. You will never be alone while in this building from check-in to checkout."

Mark presented the required key he had for the drawer in the cabinet, and the senior duty guard presented the other. They unlocked the drawer containing the keys to the execution room. Mark, Mike, and two officers walked a short distance down the hallway past some offices but did not enter the cell area, which housed the prisoners. They came to a room a short distance at the end of the hall, and the guards used the two keys from the drawer to unlock the door. Mark and Mike entered.

In front of Mike was the gurney where the subject would lie down. The condemned would come through a door at the opposite end of the room. Mike had not anticipated the size of the room and had never given it much thought. It was small, not bigger than a den or a small sitting room. No one would see where he was, as he would be behind one-way glass at the head of the gurney. He stared at the gurney and room and had an eerie feeling. He had never been in an execution chamber.

"Let's go through this door, which leads to the room where you'll prepare the drugs used," Mark said. "The prep is procedural. I'm going to go through it step-by-step, and in the end, no one will know who the executioner is. I will orient you and explain it all later."

Mark went through the entire procedure for the setup, and Mike stood quietly without asking any questions.

"Mike, you seem so quiet, you look a little pale, and you're not saying anything. Everything okay?" Mark asked.

"Yes, it's just …just … I just … I can't describe my feelings right now." He felt he was engaging in a premeditated murder.

"I think I know how you feel. I felt the same way when I started this."

With the tour and orientation over, they walked back to the guard desk, locked the keys in their places, scanned their ID cards, and walked out of 21 with neither one saying a word.

Mark stopped and gently put his hand on Mike's shoulder.

"I know this must be a jolt to you, not having been in this building or room before. Remember, you will never be alone. You will prepare; staff members will inject. You are not the executioner. The staff members are not the executioners. No one will know who injected the three chemicals that will have completed the sentence and caused the death of the condemned, not even the people doing the injecting. It will all become clear to you when we work together on your first one. You will, in time, become anesthetized to the death of this person in a manner directed by the court. It's the penalty for what they have done." Mark continued, "Just remember. You are not the executioner. The state is."

◎◎

When Mike finished for the day, he went to the Pilot. He put both hands on the wheel, stared forward, and thought about his past; he just thought. The protocol of all the keys, the dual unlocking of the doors, the fact of not being alone in the building—all these procedures came to his mind. It was all so clandestine but so inclusive. He also realized he would not be alone in this. What if someone was innocent? The thought of his anger over the years came to his mind. This new assignment could be "get even time." He decided to drive home and just reflect. But then, maybe that wasn't the best thing to do right now. A call to Carrie would be better. He needed and wanted some companionship, but he decided to do it later. He knew he loved her; he knew it.

After arriving home, Mike put on his running gear, tucked his iPhone and earbuds into his pocket, and started off for the river walk. He ran about halfway around the running path and found a quiet spot to sit down, look at the river, and to listen to one of his tapes. He found the one about "anger." He had listened to it several times before over the years and nearly had it memorized. He knew he had antagonism still inside him. He also knew these forces still waged battle within him. He'd been raised by a grandmother who loved him and whom he dearly loved, but life's circumstances had torn from him the opportunity to know either of his real parents. He'd had successes in life, and he was proud of them. Yet his mother had been tragically taken from him when he was only four years old. What would his life have been like if she had lived? What if he'd had a father present? And now, his grandmother was gone, and he had no family members—no one to celebrate his successes with. He was alone, with no net to catch him should he fail. And now he was faced with the possibility of participating in the death of a person. He was an only child with no relatives. All of these emotions lay heavily on his mind. He finished the tape and went home.

Back at his apartment, he called Carrie. He wanted to go for a walk and talk. She wanted him to join her at her place for cocktails and dinner, but they had to go shopping first.

The call that she was ready came at twenty past five. Mike drove over to her apartment. She was waiting at the front door.

She jumped into the Pilot and said, "So where are we going?"

"My place," Mike answered. "Would you approve?"

"Well… I was planning on you coming to my apartment, but I love your condo, and its large balcony. The magnificent view and sunset will be spectacular on such a beautiful day."

Mike gave her a pleasant smile and squeezed her left knee. He felt better already.

"And sometimes you come up with the biggest surprises," Carrie added.

They stopped at the local co-op, which offered a good assortment of fresh produce, as well as steaks, chicken, fish, and anything else you could want.

"I meant to stop for groceries earlier, but decided to let you have a choice. Would you like a piece of flounder or a steak?" Mike pointed to the assortment of quality meats.

They decided on a sirloin, fresh vegetables, and fresh fruit with cool whip for dessert.

"The last time I was at your place, we had the panna cotta. It was delicious, light, and a tasty finish to a meal."

Mike only smiled.

"Oh, really? I don't remember the panna cotta," Mike replied with a smirk.

They returned to Mike's apartment; he fixed a scotch and water. They went out on the balcony to watch the sunset, and Mike told Carrie everything he had learned about his new position—down to the detail of the keys.

They fixed dinner. The dessert tasted delicious.

41

Mike's alarm woke him at six. He looked over at Carrie, and they gave each other a kiss. They both knew they had to get up. He had to get her to her apartment in time to get ready for work. He would be coming to work later than usual. He made some coffee in the Keurig.

The ride to Carrie's apartment was pleasantly quiet but not tense. They looked at each other and smiled. There was a great amount of affection displayed on the way. Upon arriving, they kissed, and she left to get ready. They couldn't take their eyes off each other.

"I love you, Carrie."

"I love you too, Mike."

He opened the door for her and walked her to the front door. He had to report at ten, so he would drive back to his condo and clean up.

Before he did anything, he went to his computer and sent Aaron a message:

> *Hey, Aaron.*
>
> *Good Morning! I've been thinking of you often and wonder how you're doing. I hope you are well in whatever way one can expect. I've had a busy fall, and with winter fast approaching, I can feel the coolness in the air each morning. Besides, the days are getting shorter.*
>
> *Would you be up for visitors? I have some vacation*

days coming I need to use and also would like you to meet the future Mrs. Gibbons. Her name is Carrie O'Leary. You told me some time ago I should marry an Italian. How's that name? Yes, I am getting married and would like to bring her with me to meet you and Maria. Lemme know.

We would rent a car and stay at the Comfort Inn, where I stayed when I first arrived in Tampa. It's convenient to everything, and I'd like to go back on campus just to walk around and show Carrie where I studied. Also, a visit to St. Ben's would be in order.

Hi to Maria. We'll plan on what's best for you.

Mike

He closed the computer and had another coffee. He shaved, picked up his small package with the key in it, and thought of what it unlocked and its contents. He shook his head and pursed his lips. *I'm sorry. I wish I didn't remember.*

He showered and dressed in his uniform for work, grabbed a piece of toast, another cup of coffee, and went to his car. He would have some time to eat more in the cafeteria before reporting to his work area.

Carrie walked into the cafeteria, and they sat together. The conversation turned to the previous evening, and Carrie encouraged him not to get down about what he would be doing in 21. He spoke openly and freely with her and told her he would give it a fair try. He thought the job might help him deal with, and maybe get rid of, his personal anger.

Mike finished his usual busy day, but with no new admissions. It usually happened that Mondays and Thursdays became the busiest. The other days, he liked the quiet time, which allowed him to catch up with his paperwork data and thinking.

He went home, wanting some free time to run and relax. When he logged onto his computer, he found a reply from Aaron:

Mike

Great to hear from you, and I'm so glad you're planning a trip to Tampa. We can't wait to meet your future. Congratulations!

I'm doing okay, just okay. I take it day by day. Some days are good, and some days are not so good. I know I'm getting weaker, but I get out and walk an hour each day or try to. It keeps me going. I've lost weight. I think I might surprise you when you see me. Nevertheless, we'll still recognize each other.

Maria keeps trying to get me to eat more, but I have no appetite. I think the meds I take have done little to help me, but I would only know if I quit taking them.

If you can, come on a Saturday, any Saturday. I have a doctor's appointment every Thursday, so by Saturday, I would have updated information on my prognosis, as if I don't know what it will be. Let me know your plan. I will enjoy seeing you again and meeting Carrie.

By the way, I never received a copy of the essay you wrote from our interviews. If you have a copy, I would enjoy reading it.

Best,

Aaron

Mike wrote back, telling Aaron he and Carrie would plan to come down, but had to check with their supervisors first. They would plan to be free the entire weekend. He had been the setup person for three executions thus far, but he did not want to talk about them. He was still in a quandary about continuing the job. The trip to Tampa would be a good time to relax, get some sun, and see the man he believed was his father. He would bring a copy of the interview.

Mike received permission to take a few days off, and Carrie had some vacation days she wanted to use, so they planned to fly to Tampa in two weeks. He could get an extra day off after talking to his supervisor, who understood. He told him he'd just found out his father was dying, and he needed to visit. Leaving on Saturday would allow them to return on Tuesday and get back to work on Wednesday morning. The extra day would not be a problem for Carrie.

42

The Saturday morning two hour and thirty-minute flight was uneventful, just the usual peanuts and coke. All Mike could think about was, he was on his way to see his father for the last time. He had convinced himself a long time ago it all added up; Aaron was his dad. All the ingredients pointed to a strong possibility—the timeline and Aaron being at the University of Michigan during the time period when his mother conceived, Mike's growing up in southern Michigan not far from Ann Arbor, their shared left-handedness, and their physical similarities—blue eyes, blond hair, same height. The likeness was striking. Even their voices sounded similar.

The Northwest flight arrived on time in Tampa. After claiming their luggage and picking up the rental car, they drove to the Comfort Inn. It was déjà vu. The idea of taking a tour of the university was prominent in his mind.

After a quick lunch, he wrote a note to Aaron:

> *Hey, Aaron.*
>
> *We're here. What's your schedule?*
>
> *We have two days after today, Sunday and Monday, We'll be leaving late morning on Tuesday.*
>
> *Give me a call at the inn. We'll be out this afternoon, so leave a message if we're not here. We want to go to the*

campus, take a walk, and then go for a run by the river. I also want Carrie to meet my friend Sylvia. She's a sweet lady and a great cook.

Looking forward,

Mike

The day was pleasant, sunny, and warm. It was good to be back and a great day to go to the university campus. The warmth felt good, and Mike and Carrie walked into several buildings where he'd had classes. It was fun. The place even smelled the same, like someone had cleaned it with chlorine bleach, but he didn't see anyone he knew.

He noticed his adviser, Dr. Bob Greene, was no longer in the directory listing. Maybe he'd retired. He walked to his office and found someone else there. The room was tidy, neat, clean, and didn't smell like an old used bookstore, with a carpet on the floor and curtains on the windows. He asked about Dr. Greene, and the person told him he'd died a year ago. It saddened Mike, as he had liked Bob. *Who's next in my life?* he thought.

It made him more aware of the three people whose deaths by lethal injection he had been a part of. He'd had several dreams about them and even heard their voices in his head. It disturbed him, and he wondered if he could keep this new job. It was uncomfortable for him. The voices come without anything triggering them.

Come January, he would be on his own, without supervision. Mark's retirement would leave him as the man in charge of the preparations. He decided to give it a year, and if he felt the same way by next fall, he would advise the warden.

Mike and Carrie spent the rest of the day roaming and shopping. They made a stop at St. Ben's, and Carrie was fascinated with the work being done there. When they returned to the inn, Aaron had called and left a message. He wouldn't be available until the next morning, Sunday, and he wanted to have breakfast alone with Mike, meeting at nine at the IHOP. He apologized for not including Carrie, but they would meet Monday evening with Maria joining them.

Mike called Aaron and left a message, confirming his proposed schedule. Breakfast would be great tomorrow at the IHOP, and he looked forward to seeing Maria again. He thought she was different than other women he knew. She was pleasant and beautiful but reclusive and introvertish.

The rest of the day for Mike and Carrie would include a run by the river and a stop at "the C & P" (the Coffee and Pastry Hut) and just relaxing. He looked forward to seeing Sylvia again. He thought maybe it was time to try the scone with clotted cream as she had once advised. Also, he was excited for Carrie to meet Sylvia.

The river walk was it's usual busy place. It was now going on three on a sunny afternoon. Mike's thoughts went back to the days when his grandmother would hold off dinner until he went for his late afternoon run. It was his time of day. The thought of Nancy Moore also crossed his mind. He would be carrying out her sentenced murderer's penalty in January if there were no delays. Mike would be on his own as the "preparer." This bothered him because John Logan had always claimed his innocence. After all, his conviction was based mainly on two people claiming to have seen him running from Nancy's house that evening. It was dark, but his fingerprints and DNA had shown up on her arm and the broken glass.

His thoughts then turned to the C & P, as he saw people sitting on the patio having an afternoon cup of coffee. They entered, and he immediately saw Sylvia behind the counter. She did not see him, so he walked up and said, "Hello there."

Sylvia turned around, and a surprised look came over her face.

"Well, I nevah. Hello to you. It's been some time. What brings you here?" Sylvia's demeanor showed she was excited to see Mike. She came over to Mike and gave him a big hug.

"I came just to introduce you to Carrie, my bride to be."

The Day Always Comes

"Lovely." Sylvia looked at Carrie and let out a bit of a squeal. "I knew Mike would someday find a beautiful woman to share his life with, and I must tell you, I am not disappointed."

"Well, thank you," Carrie said. "Mike has spoken of you often, and it is such a pleasure to meet you."

"But more so than just an introduction, I came all the way from Ohio just to have one of your scones and clotted cream. I hope they aren't all sold out."

"Sold out!" Sylvia smiled with delight. "I have saved the best one just for you. I shall get it straightaway."

Sylvia went to the baked goods case and picked out the best scones she could find. She stopped at the cooler and picked out a small jar of clotted cream. "And will you be having tea with it?" she asked.

"Oh my, I have never learned the British way. Not tea. I would like a cup of your Columbia, no cream."

"Coffee with a scone? Wicked! I've told you before, in England, you have tea with your scone. Carrie, you have some work to do."

Carrie responded with a smile and said, "I'll get to work on it, straightaway as you say."

"Well, I am delighted," Sylvia said with a hearty laugh.

"Well, I'm not a tea drinker," Mike quipped. "I prefer coffee. Now isn't that Scilly?"

"Oh my, you looked it up. How lovely." Sylvia and Mike laughed as if it was their private joke and not a joke known throughout England. Sylvia continued, "I can see I still have even more work to do with you. I only enjoy coffee after my evening meal and only one cup, decaffeinated, of course. Now I shall want both of you to enjoy this with my compliments."

"Sylvia? You are so sweet. I thank you, and I shall nevah forget you.

"No, you shant. It is so good to see you, and I shall nevah forget you, either. However, you need to work on your British accent." They laughed. "Good to see you again, and to meet Carrie. All the best to you both." Sylvia came around the pastry case and gave them both a big hug.

Mike smiled, "Good to see you as well, Sylvia, and all the best to you. Cheers!"

"And cheers to you both."

Mike took his coffee, scone, and clotted cream out to the patio.

43

It was eight fifty-five, and Carrie decided to sit by the pool while Mike and Aaron met. He sat at a table near the window and saw Aaron's car pull into the parking lot. When the door opened, Mike could not believe what he saw when Aaron stepped out. Here was this thin man, walking with a cane in his right hand and wearing his Detroit Tigers cap and his iridescent Ray-Bans. His gait was slow as he lifted his legs to step over the curb. He immediately saw Mike sitting at the table and raised his left hand in a greeting.

Mike stood up as he entered. "Aaron, I can't tell you how good it is to see you."

"And you as well. Look at you. Fit and handsome as ever."

Mike smiled and gave Aaron a big hug. "Sit down. Breakfast is on me, and you'd better eat all of it."

Aaron smiled. "Well, you still have that firm grip of a handshake, I must say. I remember the first time we met at St. Ben's. You told me you were a high school wrestler and coaching at a high school while you also wrestled at the university just for fun."

"That's right. I remember meeting you for the first time as well."

"I can't think of anything I'd rather not do than wrestling at this point. I'd be toast in less than five seconds."

"I'd go easy on you," Mike said, laughing.

Mike and Aaron continued to talk while enjoying their breakfast. Aaron wanted to know all about Mike's bride to be and his new position at the prison.

Aaron looked at Mike, smiled, and said, "You are so much like me. I see you like a clone of me in younger years, and that's a compliment."

"I know. I've thought about our similarities so many times. It's ironic. There must have been a mold of you left over."

Aaron and Mike both smiled and decided it was time to get going. Aaron had some "Aaronds," to do, as he always called them, and would meet Maria later. They agreed to meet Monday evening at seven. Mike paid the bill, and he and Aaron got up from the table. He noticed how gingerly Aaron got up. He had to push himself up, as he didn't have good strength in his legs. He did need his cane and showed a weakness Mike had not seen before. Aaron's health had deteriorated.

༺༻

Monday evening, Mike and Carrie met Aaron and Maria at an outdoor café on Westshore Boulevard. It was wonderful to meet Maria again. She wore a simple, yellow dress, and the scent of her perfume was captivating. The conversation focused on times past. Both Aaron and Maria thought Carrie was beautiful and expressed their opinion of Mike's good taste. The discussion moved from Mike's time in high school on the wrestling team to his stint with the Navy and on to his college years at the university, his meeting Aaron at St. Ben's, and where he was now.

Mike did not expand on the job he did in building 21, and no one asked. He told Aaron and Maria he worked in admissions and told some of the stories of various prisoners entering the prison.

The evening conversation encompassed the entire table; it wasn't just woman to woman and man to man. The meal ended with coffee and crème brûlèe. The four of them walked out into the parking lot and stopped at Aaron and Maria's car. Mike and Aaron walked a slight

The Day Always Comes

distance away from Maria and Carrie. They smiled at each other and gave each a big hug. Mike hesitatingly said, "Good-bye … good-bye."

Aaron's eyes filled with tears, and he could hardly speak. He just stared for a moment. "Good-bye," was all Aaron could say as they shook hands with each other. He continued staring at Mike, and a moment later, he said, "We are so similar in looks—our hair, our height, our left-handedness—and in so many other ways." Meeting Mike's gaze, he added quietly, "Although I do not know if I have a son, as I've told you in the past, if I did, I think you are the son I would want."

The reality had sunk in for both of them.

Mike had never told Aaron how his mother had brought him into this world. But it suddenly didn't seem to matter. Both he and Aaron were acutely aware of the connection between them?

Mike smiled and walked over to Maria and gave her a big hug. "What is the perfume you are wearing, if I may ask?"

"It's Chanel No. 5, Aaron's favorite."

"It's wonderful and suits you well. I might get some for Carrie for Christmas." Mike added, "Take good care of this guy. He means a lot to me." Then he paused.,"I know you will."

Carrie expressed how good it was to meet Aaron and Maria and gave them both a hug.

They left. Mike could hardly believe how the evening ended. Carrie and Mike went back to the motel to pack so they would be ready to return to Ohio the next day. Mike thought, *Maybe I should just be at peace and leave it to rest. I am convinced of my feelings.*

The executions and preparations didn't sit well with Mike. He complained to Carrie how he could see the condemned in his head and hear their voices. There was something about the prisoners. After all of the executions, he would come home to a scotch, or maybe even a martini. The drinks relaxed him. He dreamed about what he was doing, and he tried not to let it bother him. Their voices would come to him and remember seeing their last breath. He told Warden Barba about his feelings. The warden asked him to stay with it. Mike said he would.

The winter months came with cold and snow. It reminded him of growing up in southern Michigan, but where he was in Ohio had a greater lake effect, which meant more snow.

The work continued at the prison. How could so many be committing crimes? He admitted men from petty to violent. Some would spend only a few months or several years, while others would be there for the rest of their life. He received greetings at Christmas from Warden Barba and his family, but none came from Aaron and Maria. The last he had communicated with them was just after Thanksgiving. Mike had gone with Carrie to meet her family on two separate occasions. Each time, he had taken Carrie's mother flowers. They heartily approved of him, and a May wedding was planned.

Aaron had known this Christmas would be his last and said in his e-mails he hoped he would be there to celebrate it. Mike wondered whether no news was good news.

In mid-January, Mike received a letter from Maria telling him Aaron had passed away on January 4. He had made it to Christmas.

Mike knew, when six months went by, he would have the letter he had long been waiting for—the letter telling him Aaron was his father.

44

Twelve years had passed. During all that time, John Logan and his attorneys worked aggressively, filing appeal after appeal, followed by denial after denial. The Supreme Court refused to hear the case, and the moment had arrived; John's day had come.

Warden Barba went through the execution chamber and inspected everything to be sure it was ready, including the witness and preparation rooms. Mike was there, and all was a "go." With the inspection completed by Warden Barba, he left to meet John Logan at his holding cell and escort him to the death chamber. The gurney in the center was ready, with the straps placed in line where John's arms and legs would be secured at several points, including the wrist, elbow, knee, ankle, abdomen, and chest. There were six correctional officers standing in specific positions around the perimeter. The floor was gray linoleum; the walls were white ceramic tiles halfway up, with institutional green painted the rest of the way to the ceiling. In a few moments, John Logan would receive a lethal injection for a murder he had repeatedly said he did not commit.

An hour earlier, John made his confession to his friend Father Jim Fischer, stating what he had said many times. The prison personnel stood next to them and heard everything.

Father Jim looked John straight in the eye. "John, I have known you for a long time. We were friends, playmates, classmates, and grew up together. You have been a wonderful friend, and I believe you. I have always believed you. I know you are the wrong man going to your death, and there is nothing anyone can do about it." Father Jim went on to give John absolution and prepare him for his eternity.

They embraced; John sobbed loudly. He stood up and walked with Warden Barba and four other prison personnel to a door down the hall. Father John followed.

John Logan entered the brightly lit room at five-fifty. John squinted because of the brightness. Two guards were holding him, followed by four others. He looked at the gurney and slumped down, turned his head from side to side as if *no* was the only thought in his head. His face showed the fear of what was to happen, but he also showed a manner of acceptance. He knew there was no escape and did not struggle. He looked pale and thinner than he had thirteen years ago when he'd entered building 21. His face was gaunt, with a light stubble adding darkness to his chin. The black hair covering his head was now short, thin, and graying. The dark circles of his eyes accented his face, making them appear sunken and cold. John had aged dramatically and didn't look like himself—at least not the John of the past.

He entered the room wearing a short-sleeved white jumpsuit, at least two sizes too large. The slippers on his feet were the only items that fit his body.

John approached the gurney and stopped momentarily. Six guards quickly moved toward him in a rhythm that resembled a clamshell closing. They immediately laid him down, not forcefully but quickly, and he did not resist. The guards, all wearing rubber gloves, were deliberate and methodical. Two of them strapped John's legs in place, two secured his arms, and two placed the heavy leather over his abdomen.

The warden nodded to two men standing at the end of the gurney. They came forward. They were medical personnel, also wearing rubber gloves. They applied a tourniquet to each bicep, wiped John's arms with alcohol and inserted a needle into a large vein in each arm. They lowered each IV bag of saline solution below the level of the gurney to see if blood would backflow. It did. They hung each bag on a double hook, its top shaped like a T, and attached to a rod at the head of the gurney. They put leads from a heart monitor on his chest. Death would occur when the monitor went "straight-line," and the medical personnel moved forward, listened with their stethoscopes, agreed, and pronounced him. They attached two lines from each IV, leading to one small opening in another room with a one-way window observable only from the inside. Everything was ready. A guard opened a curtain to a room where the twelve witnesses sat. Dianne, John's wife, and their two daughters were not there. They had said their emotional and tearful good-byes earlier that afternoon.

Asked if he had any last words, John turned his head toward a microphone and said, slowly and deliberately, with a rigid jaw, "I am innocent!"

No one seemed moved by his statement. Some acted as if they hadn't even heard him.

According to protocol, the warden read the execution order signed by a judge. He then looked over at the red phone on the wall directly connected to the governor's office to see if a light was blinking. It was not. It was six sixteen.

He folded the papers, placed them in his suit jacket pocket, buttoned his coat, and straightened his necktie. This was the signal to start the release of the three chemicals. No wave of the hand or nod of the head, just straightening the tie—the signal to begin.

Earlier, Mike had prepared six syringes. Three contained the necessary chemicals; three contained normal saline. Each had a color top—one red, one green, and one yellow. With Mike out of the room, a guard with another present, shuffled the syringes between the two injection stations. He called in the personnel who had left, and the guard who shuffled the syringes then left the room. No one now in the room would know which were filled with lethal chemicals and which were filled with saline. The guard then called in the two prison personnel who would begin the injections. The red pair would be first and would render John unconscious. The second pair would stop his breathing, and the third pair would stop his heart.

Mike was returned to the room. Having received the signal, another guard told the personnel to start the injections. They would be one minute apart. The people behind the one-way glass emptied the six syringes as directed, leading to the lines in John's arms.

Moments later, John let out what sounded like a cough. Four minutes later, the heart monitor went 'straight-line,' showing no heartbeat. The medical personnel came forward, placed their stethoscopes on John's chest and nodded, agreeing. John Patrick Logan was pronounced dead.

45

The cough stirred John. He suddenly felt a rush over his body. It was like standing under a cool waterfall. Faster and faster, he moved with a cleansing feeling and into the bright light. The execution chamber became brighter than before and visible to him. He recognized everyone. He felt relieved, refreshed, and free. The cardiac monitor showed cardiac rhythm stopped. He rose above the room and heard the words, "Time of death: 1832." He saw a guard close the curtains outside the observer's room. Father Jim moved forward, placed his left hand on John's chest, blessed him and said, "May the eternal light shine upon you. May the angels take you into paradise; may the martyrs meet you at the gate. Rest in peace … my dear friend." He moved back and left the room while the personnel removed the needles from John's arms. They put a gauze pad and Band-Aid at each insertion point and moved his body to a shroud on another gurney. They wrapped him, tagged the big toe on his right foot, and wheeled him out of the room. John Logan was dead.

Where am I? John exclaimed out loud, but no one could hear him. *This is so beautiful, so peaceful. I remember singing at Mass, "All That Is Hidden Will Be Revealed." And it was.*

John stood before a multitude of people. The brilliant light gave him peace and tranquility. In the congregation of great numbers, John saw his parents slowly coming toward him at a gate. His mom and dad had been eighty-six and eighty-eight when they'd died, but they looked young and healthy. Their bodies were glowing, and they smiled while reaching out in a welcoming gesture. His sister, Leslie, who'd died of ovarian cancer at age forty-three, was standing close to their parents. No one spoke. As John moved forward, he recognized Nancy Moore. She was resplendent and beautiful. She held out her hand in an expression of appreciation to John. They had all gone before him. They were beautiful, glowing, and shining brightly. Their movement appeared slow and deliberate, as if in pantomime.

I can see all, John thought as he saw the universe. *There's the school I attended, my university, my church. I see my school friends and the people who accused me. There's my home. Dianne is still there. And I see our daughters, one married and both grown and flown. I also see the two grandchildren I never met. I see Nancy's house. A car is in the driveway; it isn't Nancy's. The house must have sold. Everything is so clear now; I know who killed her.* He recognized other people he knew on earth—his friends; Father Jim. There was no day, night, or passage of time; only the joy of being free.

John went to Dianne as she was sleeping. He laid down on the bed where he slept each night of their marriage. He could hear her breathing, the funny noises she always made. He smelled her body with its scent of lavender bath oil, which she often used at night before bed. He touched her, but she did not respond. He saw his wedding ring resting on the nightstand with hers.

John saw Dianne awaken with a start. She sat up straight. She looked over to where John once slept, the space unruffled and the pillow fluffed and in place. She looked around the darkened room with only the night-light brightening the outer hallway. Dianne sniffed and moved her head slowly from side to side. She smelled something. "Calvin Kline. John?" Tears rolled down her cheeks as she raised her knees to her chest, rested her arms on them, and placed her forehead on her folded arms.

"Why did this have to happen? You didn't deserve it."

Dianne laid back down, wiping tears from her eyes.

John said to Dianne, *I'm happy. I'm okay. I know who murdered Nancy Moore.*

Dianne didn't react.

46

John Logan had been on Mike's mind almost constantly. He'd been having difficulty sleeping, with nightmares awakening him as he dreamed about John Logan and the house on Chestnut and Grand. Now that he'd been the one to prepare the lethal concoction that had taken the man's life, it had gotten worse. In his mind, he kept hearing, *Why did you kill me?* The question had been repeated over and over since the moment of Logan's death by lethal injection. He'd heard it throughout his drive home, and he heard it again now as entered his apartment at Summit Towers.

The January night was cold, with a light snow still falling. It was nine-thirty-two. Mike continued to do what he always did after leaving 21. He went to his refrigerator, took out a cold bottle of vermouth and gin and a correct martini glass from the freezer, placed about a teaspoon of the vermouth in the frosted glass, swished it around, and dumped it out. He filled the glass with cold Bombay Sapphire gin, his favorite. He enjoyed his "in and out" martini. The garnish was always two olives, preferably stuffed with blue cheese, though plain olives would do in a pinch; but always two.

Enjoy it while you can, John said. *You are responsible for setting up for my death, and someday, that martini will be your last.*

He watched Mike take off his work uniform, loosen his tie, unbutton his white shirt at the neck, and kick off his shoes. Mike sat down in his favorite leather La-Z-Boy, pulled the side lever back, reclined slightly, looked out the front of his ceiling-to-floor windows at the city lights with the light snow falling and relaxed in the dark. He took a sip of his martini.

Why did you kill me? John asked.

Mike jerked his head slightly, squinted, and moved his head to the side.

"What a day," he said out loud in a soft voice. "I'm not sure I can take much more of this." Doing the prep work meant a significant pay raise, and, like anyone else, he could use the money. However, he never felt comfortable.

A few months before John Logan's execution, Mike started to feel some guilt. The house on Chestnut and Grand—he could see it clearly as if he had just walked past it. He told people he worked at the prison in administration, and technically he did. Mike felt guilt over John Logan's death.

Mike sat in his chair and couldn't get the evening off his mind. He thought of all the executions he had prepared, and he realized he could not continue. He hated to lose the money, but that wasn't important to him. He thought of the preparations, the watching of a person taking his last breath, the medical personnel pronouncing. The thought that he'd personally contributed to the death of a person was equally disturbing. Mike sat in the dark, took another sip of his martini, clenched his fist, and talked out loud to himself.

"Tomorrow, I'm going to talk with the warden and see if I can change positions."

Why did you kill me if you thought I was innocent? John asked again.

Mike closed his eyes and moved his head from side to side.

John was holding Mike personally responsible for his execution, even though his death was the result of many people—lawyers, detectives, juries, judges.

Mike was halfway through his martini when his cell phone rang. The caller ID showed it was the warden. Mike answered. "Hello, this is Mike."

The voice on the other end was gravelly, the sound of a smoker with emphysema. The sound was especially prevalent tonight.

"Hey, Mike!" the warden exclaimed in an excited voice. "Good job tonight. This was one of the most controversial, and you did clean work. You had it ready, and there was no interruption or delay. I like it when it goes without a hitch. You've caught on quickly. I like working with you." It was as if the warden enjoyed these events. Mike sensed the smell of stale tobacco smoke even though they were on the phone.

Yeah, John said. *You killed a man. That's what you call clean work!*

Mike hesitated, looked around the dark room, and stared out the window.

"Mike, you still there?" the warden asked.

"Yeah ... Oh, yeah! I'm sorry. I thought I heard something." Mike continued, "I have some reservations, Warden, and I'm not sure I can continue doing this. The man I set up and whose death I witnessed tonight might have been innocent. I believe it, but I don't know why. I need to talk to you in the morning."

"Whoa! Wait a minute, Mike. Just remember what I told you when you started this job. You can't let this override your feelings and emotions. It's a job, and the state is doing the execution, not you. We'll talk more in the morning. We have another one coming up in a week. I just wanted to call to say you did it just right. Very professional."

Mike hung up his phone, laid it in his lap, and said out loud, "Yeah. I do the dirty work and set it up for the state to do the killing. It's like when Eve said, 'The serpent made me do it.' There's always someone else to blame."

Why did you kill me when you thought I was innocent? John asked.

Mike put his left hand to his head, cupping and rubbing his forehead as if he had a severe headache. He remembered at the first meeting of day two of his employment when Warden Barba said, "You will not be in a position you don't like. If you do not want to be in the particular area you've been assigned to, and there is another position available, you can request it."

The day always comes, John whispered.

Mike put his half-finished martini glass and phone on the table next to his chair. After a few moments, Mike looked at the time and realized the ten o'clock news would be coming on. He turned on the television, and the first news of the night was about John Logan, filmed in front of the main prison gate. The picture flashed to the state prison, where the usual protesters from both sides of the aisle were making their presence known. A large crowd on one side had candles and was singing hymns. The other side carried signs, shouting, "Woman killer, you got what you deserved!" they chanted. The commentator was on camera giving the news story. Behind her, the gates of the prison opened. A white hearse left with the remains of John. Seen through the window was Father Jim accompanying his friend to the morgue.

There I am, Mike. That's me in the hearse. I'm there because you killed me.

Mike turned off the TV. He ate one of the olives, devoured the rest of his martini in one swallow, and chewed on the last olive.

47

The next day was not busy, but Mike felt lonely milling over in his mind what he would say to the warden. About an hour later, Mike's phone rang. It was the warden's secretary asking if it was convenient for him to come now. Mike replied he could. He left his desk. The walk seemed difficult, with his legs feeling like lead. He pondered in his mind what he would say, deciding it would be best to be straightforward and honest. He didn't want to do the work in building 21 any longer. He entered the warden's office, with Warden Barba waving him right in.

"Good morning, Mike. It's always good to see you. How'd you sleep last night?"

"Good morning, sir. It was a tough night of sleep. I couldn't get the death of John Logan off my mind. Somehow, it wasn't right."

"Mike, I told you, it isn't about you. We are dealing with the state and the courts. We must do what the law dictates. That's our job."

"I know. But I don't like it." Mike hesitated. "I do not want to be in charge of the duties in building 21 any longer. I don't want to go in there ever again."

The warden stopped, widened his eyes, pursed his lips, and turned his head slightly. He took in a deep breath to his barreled chest, coughed several times, and just stared at Mike. The moment seemed like an eternity, but Mike did not feel intimidated. He already had his mind made up.

"Would you be willing to train someone else on the procedures?" the warden asked.

"No," Mike said firmly. "As I said, I do not want to go into building 21 ever again."

"That creates a difficult situation," the warden replied. "We have two possible events coming up. We've not had a court order so far, but if you would prefer not doing it, maybe I might be able to get Mark Smyth to come back and train someone else. I do have another person in mind. Sometimes change just doesn't work out, and I know I promised you when we met during your orientation that, if you were not comfortable with your placement, we would work to put you somewhere else." Warden Barba hesitated and put his hand to his chin. "I want you to be happy here. Let me contact Mark and see if he would be willing to come back. Know that I respect your decision."

"I would appreciate it, Warden. I like the job I'm doing now. I like the people I work with, but I am not up to the work in building 21. It's not for me."

"I understand. I will do what I can to replace you. Please know this will not affect your employment or advancement in any way. There is something for everyone, and this obviously is not for you. I thank you for your honesty."

Mike smiled, stood up, and took the key to the box in 21 that the guard had given him during his orientation with Mark off his keychain. He gently placed it on Warden Barba's desk. They both stood up and shook hands, and Mike left.

The rest of the day was difficult. The voice of John Logan remained silent in his head. Mike had lunch with Carrie, and she remarked how quiet he was. He told her how much he did not like what he did in 21. He could not continue. He told her about the meeting with Tony Barba.

She smiled, "If it doesn't feel right to you, then you have to do what your conscience dictates."

It always felt good to talk to Carrie. She was great. He knew he could depend on her to always listen.

Mike left work at the usual three o'clock hour. He got in his Pilot, put his hands on the wheel, looked straight ahead, and began to weep. The strain of the work he did in 21 had caught up to him. He felt good about talking to the warden and quitting the job, but somehow, the guilt over his connection to ending a person's life would not leave him.

He started the car and drove off. Even though it was winter, he wanted to go out for a run. When he arrived at his apartment, he checked the mail and changed his clothes.

48

Summer came. It was hot, and July did not disappoint. Mike did not return to 21, and he was grateful to Warden Barba for understanding and helping him through a difficult and emotional time. Mark Smyth came back and trained someone else.

Mike met Mark in the cafeteria one noon at lunchtime.

"Somehow, I knew you would not continue," Mark said. "I could tell from the start you were not the right person emotionally for the job. You have a strong set of ethics, and you have to be passive in performing this work."

"Thanks, Mark. Yes, I did not feel right about 21 somehow. It was dealing with nothing but death. I didn't like it."

The marriage had gone well in May, and both Mike and Carrie felt good about each other. They were very happy. Carrie had moved to the condo shortly before the wedding, as her lease would expire soon. It was now the end of July, and Mike checked the mailbox, sometimes twice daily, looking for the letter he'd expected since Aaron's death, and the six-month waiting period had ended. He wished he could drive to the county in southern Michigan and receive the news directly. He made a couple of phone calls to the county clerk's office. They told him he would receive the information as soon as they received it from the records division.

Two weeks after running into Mark, Mike started to feel better, and the voices in his head had become infrequent. He also was sleeping better. Mike finished at noon and returned home from work. It was a Friday afternoon, and he looked forward to an active weekend of running, dinner with Carrie, being home with his wife, and some general R & R. He went directly from the garage to his mailbox.

It was there—the letter from the office of the county clerk, Washtenaw County, Ann Arbor, Michigan. He took the letter and let out a big, "Yes!" It was all he could say. He was so excited.

His heart began to beat faster, and the elevator couldn't go up fast enough. He was so fired up to tell Carrie when she came home. Either what he thought was true, or the search would be over. He did not want to go any further.

Mike spoke out loud as if talking to another person. "I'm gonna fix myself a scotch, sit down, slowly open the letter, and give a salute to my dad, Aaron. I've been waiting for this moment for a long time. I am gonna savor every second. The day has finally come."

Mike put the letter on the table next to his chair, changed into a pair of running shorts and a clean T-shirt, left his shoes and socks in the bedroom, and went to the refrigerator. The sound of the ice clinking in the glass was an invitation to take his time. He loved the sound. He took out his bottle of Chivas, poured about an inch, splashed it with some water, put in a slice of lemon peel, went over to his chair, and sat down. The letter opener was on the table. He took a sip of scotch, put the glass down and slid the opener into the top of the envelope. With a smile on his face, he unfolded the letter.

> *Dear Mr. Gibbons,*
>
> *In regards to the sperm donor in the insemination of your mother, Sharon Gibbons, we are able to provide you the information you requested. Six months earlier, we received notification of the donor's death. Per the donor's stipulation, we may now release his name to you.*

Please be advised that we do not have any information on the cause of death. We know only that the donor, previously referred to by donation number, is now deceased.

I hope this helps and brings you closer to closure in your search. As required by law, the donor's name will now be listed on your birth certificate as your birth father.

His last known address was:
878 Coitsville-Hubbard Road
Youngstown, Ohio 44505
The donor's name was John Patrick Logan.

Very truly yours,
James J. Herald
Office of the County Clerk
Washtenaw County
Ann Arbor, Michigan

49

John watched Mike jump up, gulp down his scotch, and go into his bedroom. It was a large room with a huge, ceiling to floor window facing the city. The metropolitan area and the afternoon sunshine made for a beautiful scene. Mike slowly walked across the room and into the bathroom to take a shower. Tears streamed down his cheeks.

Why did you kill me? John wanted Mike to feel guilty, dirty, and filthy.

Mike put his hands over his ears and let out a cry, "No! No! No! Please don't come back. Stop it! I can't believe this is happening again. This isn't the way it …it …it … This is not the way I …I … Nooooo!"

The water was hot; the soap smelled good. It was Irish Spring. John watched Mike spend a longer than normal time in the hot water, lathering up several times. He thought Mike was trying to wash away the work he had done.

Give it up, Mike. This is your father speaking. It's not going to disappear. You've made your bed, and you are going to sleep in it for a long, long time. Mike turned off the water and grabbed a big, fluffy, Turkish towel. He dried himself, folded the towel over the rack, and walked to his dresser where he kept his underclothes.

He stood in front of the chest for a few moments, looked down, before pulling out the bottom drawer. Removing the clothes, he laid them on the bed. He went back to the bathroom. It was time to retrieve

The Day Always Comes

the key he had kept in his shaving kit all those years. He picked it up and went back to the bedroom, took the remote, and put in the four-digit code unlocking the false bottom. He lifted it.

John watched him take out the eight-by-eight-by-two-inch box and slowly insert the key in the lock. Mike hesitated for a moment. He lifted the unlocked top and took out a large piece of fabric. It was a white, rose-printed scarf labeled, "Hermès of Paris," and Mike raised it with both hands. Mike fell to his knees. He pulled and yanked on the scarf as if he wanted to tear it to pieces, but it wouldn't give way. He jerked it from corner to corner with all the power his muscular body could produce.

"I didn't mean it! I didn't mean it! I'm sorry I did this! Oh please, God! I'm sorry! She came in when I was there, so I hid in the living room. I don't know why I went there. I don't know why. It was just out of curiosity to see if I could do what I did. It was nothing more than living on the edge. I didn't mean to kill her."

Mike accidently hit an empty glass on his bed stand, and falling to the floor with a crash, it broke into several pieces. It reminded him of the glass he'd heard and felt when Nancy Moore had thrown it at him. He knelt on the floor and laid his head on the bed; he cried, and his mind went back to that moment. He saw himself in Nancy Moore's house.

෴

I hear voices—a man's. Oh, how I want to disappear. I hear them talking, and he asks for a glass of water.

She comes into the living room, turns on a light, and says, "Who's here?"

I don't move.

"I see your foot. Get up."

As I do, she throws a glass at me; it breaks into a couple of pieces. "I'm calling the police!"

I run over to her grab the scarf around her neck. She tried to struggle to get it off. With my strength, she can't fight me. I kicked her leg at the back of the knee and knocked her to the floor. She's on her stomach, and my knee is on her back. She can't scream because I tighten the scarf around her neck. A minute later, she goes limp. I tuck the scarf under my shirt. I run out and down the driveway, wearing my white-hooded sweatshirt. I see two people across the street. They were looking at me.

෴

"I see it all over and over again. The same scenario has been in my mind for all these years. I took the sweatshirt to a homeless shelter and never saw it again. I kept the scarf thinking the murder weapon would not be found. Now, someone else has paid the price. I now have two persons dead because of me."

You knew, and yet you made someone else pay the price. I sat for all those years waiting and wondering if they would ever find the killer. Now I know it was you. I knew immediately after you killed me that it was you. I did not do the crime for which I was punished, but no one would listen—no one. If I had told the court I committed this crime of killing Nancy, it would have been over sooner because that's what they wanted to hear. You were free and continued on your way, enjoying life, friendships, sex, good food. Now I am free, and you are not. You will pay the price because, wherever you go for the rest of your life, you will have to take your lousy self with you. You love running. Well, run, run, and run the rest of your life and don't forget to listen to your tapes. They've done you no good! You will never escape. You are pathetic.

Stop it! Stop it! I didn't kill you. I did my job. I know what I did when I was eighteen. Do you think I have forgotten it? No, it has been with me every day. Sometimes I have awakened in the night, calling out in vivid nightmares about that night."

Mike got up from the floor and the bed. He slipped on his running shorts. He grabbed the scarf, took it to the kitchen, and went into the drawer where he kept the heavy-duty kitchen shears. *I should have done this years ago*, he thought. He laid out some newspapers and started to cut the scarf. Piece by piece, it went on the newspaper. He heard a police siren in the distance.

I wish that siren was for you. There is no escape. You may have thought you would get away with this, but in the long haul, you won't. I will always be with you.

Mike finished cutting the scarf into the smallest pieces he could. Tears ran down his cheeks. He had to stop a couple of times to wipe his face. He folded up the paper with the scarf clippings inside. He went out on his patio, opened the Weber grill, and tossed the paper on the grate. He drenched it with charcoal lighter fluid and tossed in a match. It immediately went *whoosh*, and the fire engulfed the paper and the scarf clippings.

Take note, Mike. That's where you're going to end someday, with the flames biting you in the butt. You will pay for this in a way you cannot imagine. You ruined my home, my family, my name. I wish I had never made those donations when I was at the University of Michigan, but I needed the money. No one ever knew about them. Look where it has gotten me. I just hope there are some better individuals than you out there who have the privilege of life because of me. You are going to burn like the fire in your grill for all eternity.

The fire continued and started to die down. Mike took a tool from the side of the grill and pushed the coals around. Everything burned, and the fire ended. Mike turned toward the city, the sun shining on his bare chest and face. He put his hands on the balcony railing, and with tears rolling down his cheeks, he looked down from the twenty-sixth floor.

Go ahead, Mike. It's over. Your day has come. The day always comes.

Author's Note

This book is the result of a news program I saw on television in Tampa, Florida, about twenty years ago. A person was released from death row at a state prison, having been incarcerated for a crime he did not commit. The big question for me was, what if this person had been wrongly executed? I am sure some have.

I originally wrote *The Day Always Comes* as a short story—twenty pages—for my English honors program project in creative writing at Augsburg College in Minneapolis, Minnesota, in 2009. Six years later, I decided to expand and develop it into a full-length novel. If you read my first book, *Till Death Do Us Part*, you will have met Aaron and Maria in a different time and setting. This is not a sequel. Much of the writing has changed since I started it, with many additions inserted. I found it to be more work than I planned on. It ended up as a one-year project with many "where-do-I go-from-here" moments. Sometimes I was just plain stuck, but I never gave up. My wife was very supportive and kept me going.

The Day Always Comes is entirely fiction, inspired by a real-life event. I will refer to it as "faction." Some of the names of places are real only for the purpose of giving you, the reader, a sense of location. The idea for the story was all in my thoughts. I hope you enjoyed reading it as much as I enjoyed writing it. Please know, I am bitterly opposed to the death penalty.